BoD™

BOOKS on DEMAND

Young adult-fiction

Of Bullies and Men

Dedicated to my daughter, Alexandra

Daniel Tomazic

Bibliographic information of the German National Library:
The German National Library lists this publication in the Deutsche Nationalbibliografie; Detailed bibliographic data are available on the Internet at http://dnb.dnb.de.

Originally published in German as Ein krimineller Frühling by Lulu 2008

Printed and bound by BoD – Books on Demand, Norderstedt

ISBN: 9783748182115

Chapter 1:   Boyle's law

1977

"Thomson, what's the second binomial formula?"

"Well, err, A minus B-squared equals A-squared minus two X, um... two X..." "My dear boy! May I suggest you spend a little less time daydreaming? Binomial Formulas are an integral part of elemental algebra and are a means to depicting and solving square-binomials. They are supposed to make it simpler for you to remember things! And you can't even remember that!"

George dejectedly stared at his desk. Why did Mister Brightman always have to catch him spacing out? It wasn't that he was a terrible teacher, per se, but he had this weird talent for knowing when someone didn't know something, and a terrible habit of rubbing it in in front of everyone, to go with it. Now everybody was staring at him. Some were laughing. George, Georgy, to his friends, felt like his stomach was doing somersaults and his ears were on fire. He was pretty convinced that the warmth they emitted alone would have been enough to heat the entire room.

"Tombstone, ya dweeb, been too busy drawing those dumb ship-doodles to pay attention again?" Said a fat boy with a mean, bloated face and a malicious sparkle in his eyes. His name was Philip and Georgy hated his guts. The feeling was mutual, it seemed. For a few seconds, they glared at each other across the room. 'You moron', Georgy thought, directing all his mental energy at Philip, trying to make him drop dead on the spot 'If your old man weren't some important toppa top, bribing the school whenever your dumb-butt is about to get suspended, you'd be long gone! How can one person suck so much? But then again, with a last name like Shytles, I guess it makes sense.'

The bell rang and Georgy gave a relieved sigh. School was finally over. While he was practically sprinting out of the classroom, he heard Mister Brightman say: "Homework for tomorrow: Pages 56 and 57 in your books, memorize the third binomial formula and do the exercises on the second one, which you will find on the worksheet I just handed out." And Philip tripped him on his way out the door, so he bumped his leg on a table. It hurt. Georgy spent the entire way home imagining how he'd make that turd pay. Like by filling his schoolbag with foam rubber, or covering the inside of his motorcycle helmet with black shoe polish, for instance. See how he'd like that.

Philip was a year older than him and was allowed to drive Mopeds. Unsurprisingly, his dad had gotten him one and he used it to try and impress girls. It was freezingly cold out.

It was the end of January, winter had returned with a vengeance and it had been snowing all night. Georgy made a face at the snow. Although his mom

2

always gave him the money for his monthly bus tickets, he usually chose riding his bike instead. He lived one village over and it took half an hour tops, plus he preferred using the money for other things, mostly books. His allowance wasn't all that and his parents weren't exactly rich, so he needed every cent to buy new things to read. He loved everything to do with ships and seafaring, but those books weren't cheap and he was a fast reader. The ticket cost 5 dollar and he got another 4.25 in allowance. Put them together and he could make do for the better part of the month.

On days like that one, however, he did regret it a bit – a quick bus ride sounding far more appealing than being whipped around by icy winds on a frozen street for thirty minutes – but water under the bridge and all that and Georgy lazily strolled over to his bike. His stepdad had given it to him as a Christmas present. It wasn't new, someone had picked it up off a dump, but his Stepdad was a car mechanic and had rebuilt it from the ground up. He had replaced the bottom bracket, polished the chrome parts, changed the tires, fixed the gear-switch and given it a fresh coat of paint. He knew that it was a pretty neat gift, considering how little his stepdad made. Granted, it wasn't the Bonanza-bike with the curved saddle and drum-breaks he'd asked for, but he still liked it. Georgy ignored the weird, cold feeling in his gut and hopped on.

He had a bit of a hard time getting on with his parents. He'd been born out of wedlock and then his dad had wandered off somewhere. He didn't know where to, exactly. He'd stayed lots of places as a kid, mostly orphanages and then his grandma's for two years. She lived in another state. Even after he had started school, he had spent most of his afternoons at a childcare center. Eight years ago, his mom had met his Stepdad and six years ago, his baby brother had been born. Home had only felt like home since around fifth grade and even now he still had that lingering feeling that he was the odd-one out, like he was second best, somehow. And he was different, he thought, with a tinge of defiance. Different than the rest of his family. His real father, the one he didn't know, had been the child of some rich-doctor type up city-ways, according to his mother. It wasn't like he wanted him around, he wasn't paying child support or anything, but it made Georgy wonder sometimes.

Georgy had different interests than the rest of his family – he cared little for sports or gossip. Sure, things that did interest him were pretty specific and not everybody's cup of tea, but he couldn't even talk to his family about stuff he learned at school. It was embarrassing; they always looked at him like they thought he had something to prove, so he had eventually decided to just shut up about it. It wasn't like they were stupid. He was the first member of his family to attempt a higher education and although they were proud of him for that, he felt like it was

4

creating more of a gap between them somehow, a gap that had already been difficult to bridge. In reality, he knew he could have done far better in school than he did; but not only was he a bit of a slacker but he also felt like it didn't really matter. Nobody seemed to care if he did well. In a weird way, he even felt closer to his parents when he failed. Whatever the reason for the current state of affairs, Georgy made a point of sticking to the sidelines whenever the family came together. In his heart of hearts, he knew that he probably wasn't helping the situation.

He usually distracted himself by coming up with all kinds of pranks, both simple ones and those on a larger, less legal scale. Unlike Philip, however, he was clever about it, he thought defiantly. Philip just liked breaking things. Still, Georgy had to admit that he usually got a laugh out of what the lard-head tried to pass off as pranks, mostly because they ended with the guy getting caught. Nobody had ever caught *him.* Well, except for that one time when they had pulled the trashcans onto the roof of the gymnasium. He'd spent the entire summer doing community service. Beginner's folly, Georgy thought when he laid down on his bed after lunch, armed with pen, paper and his physics textbook to try and take on homework.

Adhesion, he read, (lat. *adhaerere* "to stick"), is the state of a surface-layer which develops between two touching, surfaces if certain conditions are met.

'Great', thought Georgy, 'and this is relevant to me how exactly?' He flipped through the pages. The textbook provided several depictions of how adhesive forces worked. There were close-ups of a cobweb and a hibiscus-flower covered in a myriad of water-droplets. At least it looked cool.

Next there was a page dealing with the surface tension of water, then a paragraph further it said something about air pressure.

Georgy quietly cursed the garbage that curricula kept forcing on hapless students and went to the next page. "Boyle's law", it said in bold letters and he was just about to slam the book shut in exasperation, when a photograph caught his attention. It showed an upside-down glass, suspended in mid-air, which seemed to have a postcard stuck to its rim. What surprised Georgy most was that the glass somehow appeared to be filled with water. When he looked at the description it turned out that the card only stuck to the rim because of a combination of the forces of adhesion, the surface tension of the water, the surrounding air-pressure and Boyle's law, whatever it was.

He didn't really care how it all worked but he had to admit the idea had a strange appeal. Georgy got up, went to his desk, and began digging around the drawers for a postcard. Once he had found one, he snuck into the kitchen and took a glass from the shelf.

The next morning proved surprising in so far, that the teachers' lounge was apparently being renovated. Walter, the janitor's son and Georgy's best friend told him that they were going to redo the flooring. The old carpet was to be replaced by polished stone tiles.

Just before the first lesson of the day, Georgy went to the restroom. The cocoa he had had that morning wasn't agreeing with him. Just when he had closed the stall's door behind himself, two boys came crashing into the restroom. "Hurry.", one of them hissed at the other. "Come on, move it! Gotta get all the paper into the toilet-bowls." And judging by the scraping, tearing and squishing that followed, the boys did just that, snorting and giggling like maniacs. Georgy barely managed to contain a snort of his own. "Look at how it absorbs the water. My monster, it lives!" One of the boys said and Georgy immediately recognized his voice. It was Philip. Just then, the door was thrown open again and suddenly everyone was screaming. "You darned kids! "He also recognized that voice. "You better start running, 'cause if I get my hands on you, you won't be running no mo- Oh, but of course it's you, Shyttles. Been missin' the principal's office, I see. Well don't worry, he's gonna be right thrilled to see ya again, I'm sure." "Whatever.", Philip shot back snootily. "Like that geezer can touch me." Georgy silently agreed. Nobody could stand the principal. The old coot seemed to exist only to dole out detention, make an appearance at the culture fare that everyone knew had only been conceptualized to support his brothers catering business and play golf in his office. When their voices began to grow distant and the door fell shut, Georgy hurried out of the bathroom and after the janitor and the two boys he was likely dragging along like two unusually unattractive sacks of potatoes. That wasn't a view he was going to miss. Seeing how he wasn't lugging the weight of two slightly overweight, slightly overgrown bullies around with him, he managed to catch up to them in a matter of seconds. The janitor, Mister Woodman, framed by a boy on each side, hauling them along by their earlobes. Georgy shuffled past them, biting back a smile and trying to look natural, as he turned around to watch them go. He knew that it would probably come back to bite him, but he just couldn't not shoot Philip the most indulgent smile he could muster. When Philip noticed, his face twisted into something ugly. "Are you laughing at me, Tombstone? You think this is funny?" He hissed, only to have Mister Woodman non-verbally signal him to be quiet by yanking on his ear. "I don't know what you're talking about." Georgy said innocently. "Don't people usually start laughing when they see your face?" Philip looked like he was ready to pound Georgy into the ground right there and then, his cheeks a rosy pink but Mister Woodman would have none of it. "Get out of here, Thomson." He said tersely. "No loitering in the hallways once class starts." "Uh, yes, Sir." Georgy mumbled and started walking into the direction he'd just come from. "When I get my hands on you...", Philip muttered as they passed each other. "I'm gonna make you sorry." Georgy raised his brows at that, his grin broadening before he put on his best clueless face. He could have sworn that Philip's ears turned even more red at that and tried very hard to hold on to the feeling of triumph, although he knew that he was probably gonna get it later.

The revenge came sooner than he would have liked. When Georgy left school that day, Philip and his gang were already waiting for him. "You got me four weeks of detention, you jackass.", Philip began unceremoniously, "The geezer immediately called up my dad." "What, only four weeks?", Georgy shot back, throwing caution to the wind. He probably wasn't going to get out of that one alive anyway. "Scum like you should be in solitary confinement for the sake of public security. And I'm not sure what I got to do with it, anyway. If you're dumb enough to get caught." "You better shut the hell up before I break your teeth. ", said Philip, the eerie calm of his voice sent a shiver down Georgy's spine but he tried hard not to let it show. Philip was marching toward him, clenched fists by his sides. "Gonna make Tombstone need a tombstone." He whispered, as if to himself. He swung back and punched Georgy in the stomach with enough force to immediately knock the wind out of him. A second fist hit him square in the jaw. Just as he was trying to steel himself for a third blow, his face and torso throbbing in unison with his racing heart, a quiet voice came from behind him. "Just can't keep your hands off George, can you Philip?" The voice belonged to Georgy's friend Walter, the janitor's son. Even though he liked to joke around and always had a snide remark at the ready, he was a good friend who almost never lost his cool. "Oh, look who it is. Am I s'possed to be scared now?" Philip said disdainfully, sneering at Wally over his shoulder. "What you gonna do, Woodchuck? Swing your mop at me?" "I could go get my dad, for instance. Fancy another trip to the principal's office, Shyttles?" Concern suddenly visible on his face, Philip took a step back. "You wouldn't dare." He hissed. Wally just shrugged. "And why not? What, you gonna beat me up, too? "Before Philip had a chance to react to that – and, luckily for them, since it looked like he was about to disregard everything that had just been said and launch himself at Wally anyway, the front gate was thrown open and students began to flood the courtyard. Philip pointed a finger at them: "Oh, look at that. Lucky you, I guess. Just so you know, if we were alone right now, I'd totally pound ya. " "Noted.", Georgy said, wiped at his busted lip with one hand and dismissively waved in Philip's general direction with the other. "C'mon. ", Wally said. "You can clean yourself up at my place. "He shot a cool glare at Philip and his gang. "You better lay low for a while." He called over the hustle and bustle of kids' chatter and footsteps. "Or I might let something slip to my dad about how you're too dumb to control your mouth and fists at the same time." Philip clenched his fists again, when one of his cronies grabbed his sleeve. "Those losers aren't worth it." He said. "Come on, let's just get out of here. "

A little later, both boys were seated at the dining table at the Woodman residence and Wally's mother served them some casserole. "I hope that piece of trash gets what is coming to him one day." Wally said after they had been eating quietly for a while, the scarping of their spoons against their plates the only sound in the room. "Patience, my friend.", Georgy said. "This casserole is great, by the way. You know, at my place, there's always just pre-cooked food for lunch, 'cause my mom works late." "No sweat." Wally said with a grin. "Dig in. You wanna stick around for a while? "

And stick around Georgy did – not like there was anyone waiting for him at home, anyway. Wally and he even did their homework. Once they were done – Georgy usually just did homework at school before class, copied it off a friend or skipped it entirely – they just sat there and talked. Georgy didn't feel guilty for once without the unfinished schoolwork hanging over his head and was in high-spirits. "Man, your dad busting that Shyttles-turd just completely made my day." He said. "Yeah, pretty good of him, that." Wally agreed. "Though stuff like that kinda makes me wish he had a different job sometimes." "What? Why? And where's your dad anyway? Doesn't he usually eat lunch with you?" "Well." Wally said, making a roundabout gesture with his hands. "He spoils everyone's fun. It's not like he only busts jackasses like Philip." "Yeah, but you gotta admit that it's mostly Philip these days. Can't imagine anyone giving a damn about that." "True, most people don't – Philip and his hooligans do." "Oh." Georgy was quiet for a moment. Wally didn't usually talk about stuff like this, so it had to really have been bothering him. "Yeah, I get it." He said, giving Wally a sympathetic look. They fell silent until Wally cleared his throat. "Well, anyway..." He said. "Dad's overseeing the renovation of the teacher's lounge, or something. You know, with the new tiles." "Yeah, I saw them this morning." Georgy responded, "They do look pretty neat. Real fancy." "Fancy-shmancy." Wally snorted indignantly, rolling his eyes. "Dad says it's polished 'rose porphyry' or something and that he isn't looking forward to mopping it 'cause water makes it super slippery. Says his only consolation is that maybe all the chalk pushers fall and break their powdered noses." Snickering, they got up from the table and wandered over to Wally's room.

When Georgy looked up, it was obvious he was thinking about something. "You know what?", he said turning to Wally, "I think I've got an idea." "Yeah? What?", Wally asked, flipping through a comic book. Georgy couldn't fight back a grin. "Well, I may have figured out a way we could make our teachers 'slip-up', as it were." Wally slapped the comic shut and tossed it aside, swinging his legs over the side of his bed. "Yeah? So? Spill." Georgy's grin broadened. "That's exactly the plan."

Georgy picked up his bag and took out the physics textbook. "Lookey here.", he said, pointing at the photograph of the upside-down glass of water. Wally stared at it. "So...", he began lamely. "You finally figured out how to open a book by yourself. Proudest day of my life." Georgy snorted, only slightly offended. "Yeah, wonders never cease. Anyway, listen to this. If you flip a filled glass of water around and place it on a smooth surface, no liquid can escape." Wally still wasn't getting it. "So you learned to read, too.", he dead-panned, half-jokingly, as he pointed at the description underneath the picture. Georgy punched him in the thigh. "Aren't you funny today.", he grumbled. "Plus, I didn't need to read it, we went over that in physics, remember genius? Force of adhesion, surface tension and stuff." "Oh yeah, now I remember. Especially the stuff." "Shut-up, will you? Imagine someone, say, covered the entire brand-new stone floor in the teacher's lounge with upside down glasses of water, nothing would happen at first, right? If you tried to pick them up though, say, because you were trying to clean up the mess, you'd basically flood the entire room. Instant slip'n'slide." Wally's face lit up in understanding, but his brows furrowed almost instantly. "All right, I'm with you. Just... Where'd you get the glasses? And how'd you get the water into them?" "Already thought of that." Georgy said, nodding dreamily. "Saw that Walmart had a sale on paper cups that didn't get bought during the Super Bowl – 50 cups for a dollar, 50 cents. To get 400 cups, I'll need 8 packs, would run me five bucks, which is exactly the amount I get to buy my bus ticket each month. I'm just gonna take the bike.", Georgy said, grinning at Wally. "So, how'll you fill the cups?", Wally asked, not missing a beat. "With a syringe.", Georgy shot back just as quick. "You know that ranch next door to where I live? I once watched a doctor give a cow a shot with, like, the biggest syringe I've ever seen. He threw the thing away after and I just dug it out of the garbage. I mean, you never know, right?"

"Oh, sure.", Wally said, now grinning as well, "Stuff like that might definitely come in handy." They both laughed. "Still...", Wally added after a moment's silence. "Where's the air go? You know, when the water starts to fill up the insides, it needs to escape somewhere." "Easy.", Georgy said. "I'm just gonna poke another hole into the top, formerly the bottom of the cup.".

"Now picture this: 400 cups, all half-full, which means about three ounces per cup makes about nine gallons of water total-Even if they manage to get some of the water back out of there, this is gonna make for an impressive mess. What'd you think?" "Pretty clever. Man, why don't you do better at school? I mean you usually do rather poorly across the board there, don't you?" Georgy shrugged. "No clue. School's different than just... thinking up something. But anyway, there is one more thing..." "Yeah?", asked Wally, suddenly suspicious. Georgy mentally steeled himself. "I'd need the, uh, key to the teachers' lounge." "So you want me to...No, no chance in hell." Wally said, suddenly very pale. "Oh, come on.", Georgy whined, folding his hands in a pleading gesture. "You said yourself that it was a good plan, wouldn't that be worth al little risk?" Wally gave a deep sigh and considered for a moment. "The spare key." He said. "I'll just, uh... take it from the key box. Dad usually uses the one on his keychain." "Yeah.", Georgy said eagerly. "Betya he's not even gonna notice. And I'll give it back to you the next morning, honest. Please?" "Alright, okay. I'll do it. I mean, if my dad catches on, I probably won't get to leave this house until I get married." They gave each other a short nod and burst into laughter.

A few days later the time had come. Georgy had bought the cups. Buying all at the same store would likely have aroused suspicion. Why would a kid need 400 paper cups?

On Friday, after school had ended, Georgy had rigged the window in the ground-floor boys' restroom, to not close properly. The mechanism kept jamming and that way, he only had to push against it from the outside to get it to open. That way he had managed to break into the school after dark on several occasions. If nobody suddenly decided to fix it, it should work this time again. And it worked. Georgy had waited until everyone had been asleep and had slipped out the front door. He'd arranged his pillow and blanket in such a way that it looked like somebody was asleep under them. The night was cold and the streets were filled with enough fog that seeing would have been difficult, had it not been dark and when Georgy dragged his bike out of the shed, he felt strangely on edge. It was like being an actor in a thriller movie. Just before nightfall, he had put the syringe, the cups and a flashlight into his bag pack, had rifled through

14

his mother's cleaning supplies and secured one of her buckets on the handlebars.

Now, with the backpack safely on his back, he was riding over to the neighboring town. It took little more than half an hour until he reached his destination, cautious as he was in the darkness. Just before the clock struck one, he arrived at the school. He had parked his bike behind a corner store two minutes off campus and absentmindedly wondered whether someone would come along and steal it as he crept toward the main building. Getting in through the window proved slightly more challenging than usual, with the cumbersome bucket all but immobilizing his left arm, pressing it uncomfortably against his ribcage.

At first, he just sat in absolute silence, listening with bated breath for the sound of footfalls, of anything to indicated he had given himself away – then, he got to work.

Georgy had decided to only use the flashlight in the case of emergency, because he feared someone would be able to see the light through a window. Besides, he knew the school like the back of his hand, had even been there after dark once or twice before and would be able to make do with the dim glow of the many escape signs. Quietly, he snuck into the boys' restroom and filled it with as much water as he dared so it wouldn't spill, then carried it over to the teacher's lounge. He knew that the girls' restroom would have been closer, his arms already aching dully as he made it up the stairs but going in there just seemed wrong, somehow. And gross. He unlocked the door to the teachers' lounge with the key Walter had given him and suddenly stood there enveloped by complete darkness. 'Damn. It's like a monkey-butt in here.', he thought. The blends had been let down and what little light made it through the gaps didn't help much. Georgy turned on his flashlight and dropped to the floor, quietly hoping that no one would notice from the outside.

The floor really was clean, he noted absentmindedly, his nose mere inches from the polished tiles, it shouldn't be much of a hassle putting up the cups. His plan was to set them up in rows and work his way toward the door, so he wouldn't ruin all his hard work on the way out.

First, he poked a hole into the bottom of each cup, and then he individually dipped their rims into the bucket, so they would stick to the floor. Filling them with the syringe was another matter entirely, though, because it required a lot of sitting still and his hands to be steady.

Soon his eyes were stinging from squinting around the room and his knees were aching something fierce. The cushion he had lifted off one of the teacher's chairs, almost knocking over several cups in the processes, made it at least bearable. He had to go back down to the boys' restroom four times to refill the bucket, his arms tired and his knees protesting but then, it was done. Tired but content and with the knowledge that he'd be able to sleep in on Saturday, he gathered his affects, turned off his flashlight and legged it out of the teachers' lounge.

He was just about to turn the key in the lock, when he heard something. It sounded like footsteps and whispering coming from an adjacent corridor. Suddenly, his heart was hammering in his chest. Holding his breath, he slipped back into the teachers' lounge. What if they caught him? Had somebody noticed something? Walter was the only one who had known, so... No. No, he forced himself to take a deep breath. Walter wouldn't rat on him. Not in a million years. And Mister Woodman wasn't the type to patrol the premises at 4:30 am in the morning. No, it was far more likely that there were others like him. Somebody else who had broken in. He lay on the floor and pressed his ear against the bottom of the door. There they were, two voices, he was sure of it. Two people talking. He couldn't make out what they were talking about and so he got up, quietly opened the door and snuck out onto the hallway. His mouth felt strangely dry, there was a tingling sensation in his fingertips. It felt like his body was moving on its own accord. He reached the end of the hallway in the near darkness and peered around the corner. One of the voices he recognized immediately. It belonged to Philip. 'What's he doing here?', Georgy thought in agitation, pushing himself closer to the wall. "How much of the stuff'd you sell?", the other voice asked. Georgy was sure he had heard it before, but he didn't know where. "Not that much." That was Philip again. "'ts that s'pposed to mean? What, you want me to believe you just been carting it around in your backpack for two weeks? Hand over the dough? " A brief silence, broken only by the crinkling of paper. "What?!" The sudden anger in the strange man's voice made Georgy flinch. "Are you shitting me? You only sold one lid in two weeks?" "No, honest. That's all I sold." "Are you god-damn

17

ripping me off?!" There was a resounding smacking noise and Georgy was sure Philip had just eaten a fist. "Get away from me, you dill hole! I'll...!" "What? You'll what?", The man interrupted him. "You better god-damn watch your mouth or I'll make you wish you were never born!" "I ain't scared of you!" Philip yelled, but the tremor in his voice betrayed his fear. That moment, there was another audible punch, followed by a grunt from Philip. "There you go, you little shit. Plenty more where that came from!" Georgy, torn between fear and the need to do something – anything, quickly poked his head around the corner before thinking better of it. Very briefly, he saw the silhouette of the strange man, towering over Philip. His hair was long and slicked back against his skull and he wore a strange, thin moustache. When he swung back for another punch, something in his hand caught the light from a streetlamp outside the window. Suddenly Georgy was overcome by a feeling of all-encompassing panic and he would have liked to just run for it. Instead, he clenched his fists, digging his nails into his palms and crept away in the opposite direction, forcing himself to move very slowly until he reached the door to the boys' restroom. He ducked in and within seconds, had slipped out the window. As soon as his feet hit solid ground, he began to run. Only a few minutes later he was racing back home, paddling as fast as his shaking legs would let him.

Chapter 2   Aunt July and the sofas

With a start, Georgy woke from a bad dream. Soaked in sweat, he glanced at his old alarm clock. It read a quarter to ten. Nobody had noticed his absence the night before. He had climbed back in through the window, had gotten out of his cold, sweaty clothes and had hidden under the covers.

Falling asleep had taken forever. Exhausted as he had been, he had lain awake for hours to come, images of what had happened in that dark corridor flashing through his mind. So, he had scrunched his eyes shut and tossed and turned until he had slipped into a restless slumber.

Climbing out of bed, his head felt heavy and that dull feeling of dread he had had the night before, resettled in his gut. In the vague hope of scrounging up something to eat, he went into the kitchen. Maybe his mother had even cooked something. "Oh, so the clever Sir has finally seen fit to grace us with his presence. If ya hafta spend so much time in yer room, I hope ya at least found it in ya ta clean it, ya hear?" "Yeah, I'll do it in a minute.", he replied tiredly. Apparently satisfied, she gave a curt nod and scurried out of the kitchen. "I'm going grocery shopping.", she announced from somewhere in the hallway. He could hear her zip up his brother's jacket and the front door falling shut. His dad often worked on Saturdays, which meant he was alone at home, as per usual.

He got milk, butter and jam from the fridge and plopped down on a chair by the kitchen table with a sigh.

He had to get back to school, he thought, he needed to know what had happened. If anything had happened at all. Chances were, nobody would be in until Monday and if Philip had really been... He shook his head and took a deep breath. And he had to return the key to Wally before Mr. Woodman noticed it was gone. With all that had happened, he had almost forgotten about the water-cup prank, but he couldn't help but grin when he thought of it. Too bad he couldn't also install a camera in the teachers' lounge, to snap a picture of the teachers' faces when they began lifting the cups.

He wolfed down his food, shot gunned his milk and left the house in a hurry. That feeling of dread that hadn't let him go all morning had morphed into an outright panic by the time he reached school. There were police cars blocking access to the parking lot and someone had cordoned off the area where the older kids went for smokes. A few gawkers had gathered around the scene and were whispering amongst themselves.

Wally was one of them. Georgy was just about to call out to him, when Wally turned around, his eyes lighting up in recognition and he jogged toward him. "Is it because of Philip?", Georgy asked under his breath without missing a beat. "And how do you know that?", Wally asked in bug-eyed surprise. "You didn't-" Georgy briskly shook his head. "Of course not and I'll tell you later. Now, what happened exactly?" Wally only took a moment to collect himself. "Well, the long and short of it is that dad found him in the bushes over there.", he said, indicating the direction with his thumb. "He looked pretty bad, apparently. Like he took a beating. Half frozen to death, dad said, and the medic told us that he had some cracked ribs and that the hip joint's busted." "What busted? Busted how?", Georgy asked, his voice coming out higher than usual. Wally was good with stuff like this, with blood and broken bones. Georgy wasn't. Wally made a non-committal hand motion. "Well, broken. You know." Georgy was at a loss for words, staring over Wally's shoulder at the crime scene. There was a conspicuous reddish-brown spot on the concrete. His mouth felt dry. Wally touched his arm and motioned for to go stand behind the cycle rack. "Your turn." He said. "How did it go last night and what happened to Philip?" Georgy described what he had seen and done in short sentences. "And it's not like I could have gone to the coppers." He finished miserably. "They would have kept me at the station for breaking and entering and general mischief." Wally tipped back his head in thought. "So, what now?" He asked. "No clue.", Georgy said dejectedly. "Anyway, I gotta get home before my mom gets back from the store so I can clean my room, or I'll be in trouble. Here's your key." Georgy looked around to make sure they weren't being watched and when he was sure that no eyes were on them, he slipped the key into Wally's out-stretched hand.

While he was cleaning his room, he was again going over what had happened the previous night.

Who was that strange man and what was it that Philip had been meant to sell? What was a lid? Well, he knew what a lid was, generally but he couldn't imagine that someone would get so upset over the top of a pot or something. No, it must have been something illegal, otherwise, they wouldn't have met at school at that hour and on a weekend to boot. Philip had been tasked with keeping the classroom tidy and stocked with chalk and the like, so he had had a key. Well, it was likely dope or something. That stuff was being sold all over high- and middle schools in the entire country. That's what he had heard, at least. That would make the other guy Philip's supplier or whatever you called it. The way it had sounded, Philip was supposed to hand over the profit he had made and because the other guy thought it was too little, he had beaten him into a pulp.

A broken hip joint probably meant that Philip would be confined to bed for a few weeks at least, which would mean that the supplier wouldn't be able to make any money for a while, unless... "Georgy, we're back! How's the room doing? All clean?" Georgy flinched at his mother's voice and almost dropped the folded shirt he had been holding. "Still on it!" He called back, hastily stashing the laundry in the closet, when his little brother came careening into the room. "Look what I got!" He basically screamed with excitement. "A Big Jim doll! He even has a whip and everything!" "Good for you.", Georgy said through clenched teeth as he gave him a forced smile, when his mother poked her head in the door. "Still not done, are ya. Well, hurry it up!". "Did, uh, I get anything?", Georgy asked hopefully. "Yes, two new pairs of socks. For the life of me, I can't figure out how you go through them so fast." "No, I meant something like

22

Tony.". "George, you know exactly well that we don't have that kind of money. And aren't you a little old to play with dolls?" Georgy turned away in disappointment while Tony was sticking out his tongue at him from behind his mother's back. Of course, he thought bitterly, there's always enough money to get Tony some toys and it's not like he's suffering from a sock-shortage either. He took a deep breath, roughly shoved his brother out the door, threw it shut and himself onto his writing chair.

His thoughts trailed off again and, inevitably, found their way back to Philip and the strange man. Maybe somebody else was going to take over as dealer now. Maybe even one of Philip's cronies. The question was: Which one?

On Monday morning, Georgy left for school earlier than usual. He wanted to be there and see the teachers' reactions first-hand and spent a good half-hour just loitering about the assembly hall, trying to look as inconspicuous as possible. It wasn't like arriving early was unheard of or anything, since some kids had to rely on public transport to get to school but still. Misses Hyde, the biology teacher, was the first to arrive. She unlocked the door to the teachers' lounge, stood there for a second, quietly gaping, then went inside. Georgy was counting in his head. For a few moments, nothing happened. Suddenly, the woman came bursting back out of the room, visibly flustered and Georgy had to fight to suppress a bout of laughter, just when Wally approached him. "Hey, what's going on, what's the word around town?" He asked, wide grin on his face. "Can't say yet." Georgy replied. "Misses Hyde's already been in there but she

23

doesn't seem to be a screamer." The next person to go in was a coach by the name of Tulpov or something similar. Georgy didn't know him. He spent the better part of a second in a room before cursing loudly. "Unholy mess! If I get my hands on whoever did this...!" Georgy managed to look inside room over the coach's shoulder. The man appeared to have knocked over some of the cups with his foot. The entire floor was flooded. A few people were starting to take note of the commotion, people were beginning to whisper, and some were craning their necks to chance a peek at what was going on. Georgy could feel the atmosphere about to tip. "This is even better than I thought it was going to be.", he mumbled under his breath. Only a few minutes later, a group of people had gathered around the room, talking excitedly amongst themselves. The volume in the assembly hall had decreased threefold. "Maybe they brought the cups here with the water already frozen inside?" One of the older students suggested. "Nah, are you stupid?" His friend retorted, shaking his head. "What, you think they pulled up in a truck full of mini fridges?" "Could be." The other one shot back defensively. "Maybe they flooded the entire room and put the cups down after." A girl wondered out loud. "Oh, sure.", said the girl next to her. "And then they blow-dried the residue of the floor. You're so dumb, Stacy." "Or maybe it was aliens." Wally said quietly. "I think it was aliens." "Yeah, sure.", Georgy said, grinning. "Hey, let's get out of here. Class is about to start." "Oh, I don't know." Wally replied. "I think we got some time on our hands. Don't you?"

Sadly, their English teacher wasn't even five minutes late. "Miss Sanders?" One of their classmates, a girl with blond pigtails and a thick set of glasses began. "What exactly is going on at the teachers' lounge? Is there something wrong with the new flooring?" Miss Sanders' nostrils twitched dangerously. "You can say that again." She spat. "Some criminal individuals appear to have flooded the entire room." "Well, what exactly did they do to it?" The girl asked. "Well..." Miss Sanders took a breath. "The, uh, thing is... as it happens... we don't know. They covered the floor in cups, filled with water." "And?" A boy asked. "The cups are upside-down." Said Miss Sanders. "What do you mean, 'upside-down'?", Georgy asked, trying to look indifferent. He was going to delay class as long as he possibly could. He hadn't spent three hours crawling around on his knees for only five minutes of down-time. When Miss Sanders, looking more disheveled form moment to moment because she kept running her hands through her hair in exasperation, finished describing the state of affairs in the teachers' lounge, a murmur went through the room. People were whispering appreciatively, some were guessing as to how it had been done.

"What's a thesis? Can somebody answer that?" Miss Sanders was looking about the class. "George. How about you?" "Who's the X-O." Georgy replied absent-mindedly. "Pardon?" Miss Sanders wasn't generally an impatient person, but the events of the morning had her on edge. "George, may I suggest you pay attention for once?" She said irritably, her brows furrowed. He heard some of his classmates snicker. Philip was absent but his friends were still there. "You dumbass." The guy sitting next to Philip's empty desk called out. "You drunk or something?" His name was Kevin and when Georgy turned around to glare at him, he had an epiphany. Kevin was just like Philip broad and muscled just maybe a bit dumber than the others. He could easily be Philip's second in command. It would be just like Philip to pick someone that he would look like Einstein next to, someone who would be easily controlled. Silently, Georgy resolved to keep an eye on the guy. "Is there anybody in this room who can tell me what a thesis is? Come on people, make it snappy. Yes, Joanne?" "A thesis is a thought or statement, which has yet to be proven to be considered true."

Days went by. During recess, Georgy and Wally made sure to keep a close watch on Kevin and his friends. They pretended to be having a conversation or something, secretly keeping an eye on the other boys. Kevin wasn't like Philip. He was, as Wally had put it, a weasely scumbag. He thought he was so clever, sucking up to the teachers and got all-proud of himself when they didn't fail him. Kevin was short and stout, with close-set beady eyes and he always seemed to be hunching over. There was no doubt in Georgy's mind that he was the new leader of Philip's gang.

One of his female classmates had told Georgy that Philip wouldn't be able to come to school for six weeks. Somehow, strangely, he felt a little bad for the guy but then again he told himself, that moron had deserved it. If only he could figure out what the entire thing was about.

A week later, on a pleasantly mild day with white, wispy clouds that hung over the sky like a veil, the snow had melted away and Georgy felt like spring was finally about to return. He almost choked on his lunch, when Wally lightly pated his shoulder   in the schoolyard. "Jesus Wally, you trying to kill me." He grumbled irritably. "Suck it up and look at that!" Wally shot back. Georgy looked. He saw nothing of interest. "You know that chick?" Wally asked, subtly indicating a direction with his head. Georgy slowly let his gaze wander, just as if he were surveying the area and not looking for something specific. "No." He said after a while. "I mean, I've seen her around, I guess, but I don't know her. Why?" Wally gave a snort. "'Course you've seen her. Kinda hard to overlook." The girl was maybe one or two years older than them, standing next to Kevin and his gang, quietly chatting away. She had long hair that almost reached her hips, a pretty face and the bluest eyes Georgy had ever seen on a human being. Of course, he'd noticed her. Girls really hadn't been his thing up until this point. Lately, however, he kept catching himself looking at them. That wasn't too bad in and of itself but how he was looking and especially where he was looking, made him want to crawl into a bush when he caught himself. He glanced at the girl again. Wally definitely hadn't been wrong. The girl was wearing a rather tight, dark red jumper, blue skinny jeans, black boots and very colorful gloves. Georgy absentmindedly wondered if she was cold. Maybe he should offer her his jacket. "And now ask yourself..." Wally whispered, conspiratorially leaning in a bit closer. "What's a chick like that got to do with a loser like Kevin?" Just then, Kevin handed something to her. "I knew it." Georgy hissed, snapped out of his daydream. "I knew that Kevin had taken over for Philip!" "Regular psychic, aren't you." Wally mumbled, tugging on Georgy's sleeve to get him to move. "C'mon, let's go stand over there. Will be easier to talk." "I bet it's dope.", Georgy said, glumly staring

27

at the floor. "I'm a joker, I'm a smoker, I'm a midnight talker...", Wally sang quietly. Georgy made a face. "Honestly, Wally." He said, giving his friend a serious look. "Like, what are they going to start selling next? They obviously don't care if kids get caught with illegal stuff on them and considering what that guy did to Philip, I doubt they'd have any hang-ups moving on to the hard stuff." "So what do you want to do?", Wally grumbled in a low voice. Georgy sighed. "Don't know yet. Gotta think on it." They were quiet for a moment. "You got any plans for today?", Wally asked after a while. "Maybe we could figure something out." "Confirmation class." Georgy said dejectedly, shaking his head. "We'll visit the town museum. I bet it's gonna be a blast." "Hey, hang in there." Wally said in mock-sympathy. "Go educate yourself, so you don't have to die stupid. I hear only smart guys get into heaven." "Great, thanks for the support.", Georgy said sourly. "But I wouldn't want you to get lonely in hell."

The afternoon turned out exactly how Georgy had imagined it. The museum had been a bank once and now mostly featured old wooden furniture as it had been used on farms in the previous century. The building had been empty since they'd built a new bank a few streets over and the patriots and history-buffs of the region had rejoiced at a chance to rent the space for their exhibit.

It had only been opened a few days ago. The local pastor, Mister Flick, was of the opinion, that each and every one of his students should experience a piece of local history. Looking at the faces of the young people in the class, it wasn't hard to tell that they were already bored. Except for Georgy that was, who looked strangely elated. After about an hour in the place, he was almost getting into it. Or maybe he was going crazy. Curiosity piqued, he was looking at the exhibits. He counted six rustic looking parlors, all equipped with heavy wooden closets behind same looking seating areas, most of which were centered around dowdy plush sofas in various shades of green and red.

The rooms facing the street – though calling it a 'street' was a bit of an overstatement – were brighter than the rest and had tall windows, typically found in small banks of the time. They spanned the distance from the high ceiling to about three feet above the floor. One of them even had a latch. Probably so they could let some air in from time to time; Georgy thought when his eyes were yet again drawn by the atrocity of a couch in front of him, all carved wood and dark green velvet. Good thing you don't have eyes on your butt, he thought, glanced about the room to make sure that he was alone and strolled over to the couch. Assuming that the cushions would be soft, he let himself drop onto it. He almost cursed. Almost. Geez, he thought, fighting the urge to rub at his bum, no wonder people in old photos always look so sour, when the pastor called out to him to stop lagging behind. He scrambled to his feet and ran after the others, his but still hurting.

The way home led around the graveyard, but he usually took the shortcut through it. He was quickly making his way down the main path, when something caught his attention. At the back of the church stood a tipper truck, its back compartment filled with pipes, sticks and wooden planks. What was that all about? Were they going to wall of the graveyard to keep out vandals, maybe? He sat on a bench and watched the men at work for a while. "S'cuse me.", he called out to one of them. "But, um, are you building something?" A man, who obviously jumped at the chance to take a break from unloading the truck, turned to him with a smile. "We're scaffolders, son. The clock tower's ta be repainted and they're gonna restore the clock." "Oh, good.", Georgy said, awkwardly adjusting his posture. "You hurt, son?" The man asked. "No, no. I'm fine.", Georgy said, quickly shaking his head. "Just peachy, really. Uh, thanks for the info." In truth, his but still hurt and he somehow had managed to make it worse by moving. He quickly got up, said goodbye to the man and went on his way, inwardly cursing sofas and benches alike. They were all the same. Suddenly, a grin spread across his face and he walked a little faster.

The next day he spent recess watching Kevin with Wally again. "So, anything new?" Wally asked, grinning. "Had a good time at the museum yesterday?" "You may not believe it..." Georgy started testily, "But it wasn't really that bad." "I'm hysterical." Wally said, an eyebrow raised indicating he wasn't convinced. "Yeah, I'm telling you..." Georgy went on. "They have the most amazing sofas over there." "Oh, I get it." Wally said jokingly. "You've finally lost it." "No." Georgy shot back. "I'm just very passionate about this. Something that beautiful shouldn't be left to rot in a drab place like the museum." "I'm honestly starting to worry about your mental health." Wally said. "Well then keep your smart mouth in check for a bit so I can put you at ease. You see the benches on the graveyard and the

30

couches in the museum are equally as uncomfortable, except the couches are way nicer to look at. Thing is, way more people come to the graveyard than to the museum." He grinned mischievously. "You feelin' me? Say somebody switched them." Wally smiled as well, though he was clearly thinking about something. "Cool idea." He said. "But how is that somebody going to get into the museum? Pretty sure his friend doesn't have a key to that." "Yeah, yeah. I know." Georgy said, waving his hand dismissively. "We won't need one, we'll just get in through the window. There won't be an entry fee this weekend, in celebration of the 'grand opening'. We'll just wait for a group of people to go in, so we won't stick out that much and take a look around. There's a restroom just like at school." "I feel ya." Wally said, grinning again. "The best thing is...", Georgy went on, "That there are tall windows which can be opened as well; that building used to house a bank. That way, we'll be able to get the couches and benches in and out comfortably." "Can we carry them by ourselves?" Wally asked doubtfully. "Don't think so." Georgy said. "We'll need help." "And where did you intend to get it?" "Well, I thought we could get the gang back together. From when we picked up the concrete mixers in the development area and switched them around." Wally nodded in understanding. "Raff and Joe." He said and paused. Georgy nodded. Wally made a face. "Sure, Raff would be game but I'm not so sure about Joe. Since his mom caught him dying one of her cats red with watercolors, he's gotten kind of useless." "Well..." Georgy mulled it over for a moment. "Yeah, guess you might be right. Now that I think about it, I haven't seen him outside of school for ages. How about Olly, then?" "That'd work." Wally said, nodding.

At first, it seemed like Kevin wasn't going to sell anything that day. Georgy, Wally and their friend Ralph whom they just called Raff, sat huddled together between lessons. "So did you talk to Olly yet?" Georgy asked, shooting Raff an impatient look. "Sure did." Raff replied, smug grin on his face. "So? And? What?" Wally asked, just as impatient as Georgy. "C'mon, spill." "Oh, cool it, ye of little faith. When have I ever not come through for you? Of course he'll land us a hand." Georgy rolled his eyes. "Yeah, yeah, we're forever grateful." Wally mumbled. Raff wasn't a bad guy, a little arrogant maybe but a good friend in general. Georgy and Raff lived on the same street and had been playmates since kindergarten. Wally and Raff, however, were another matter. Raff was one of the few things that could get under Wally's skin. Still, they were friends. "Well, ask him yourself next time." Raff shot back, giving Wally a venomous look. "Geez, you guys." Georgy rejoined to cut them off. "Could you stop acting like preschoolers for just one minute? Next lesson's homeroom, right? Olly's homeroom teacher likes taking his sweet time seeing his people off, so we'll just wait for him by the staircase." Wally made a tutting noise and pointed to the door. "How about you dismount your high horse for a moment and look at that?" The other two's heads shot around as they looked over. "Oh, her again. Interesting." Georgy pursed his lips. "What's going on?" Raff asked, eyes drifting from Georgy, to Wally to the girl they had seen on the schoolyard the other day. Georgy considered for a moment, then he nodded. "All right, we'll tell you." He said. "Oh, will we?" Wally said, crooked half-smile on his face, obviously still wound up but he didn't object. While Georgy was telling his story, Raff's eyes seemed to grow a few sizes while he was continuously shaking his head in disbelief. "So... That was you." He said, chuckling, when Georgy had finished. "With the teacher's lounge. Man, I should have known." "Just like you should know how to keep your big mouth shut but you just keep running it ." Wally said scornfully. "Yeah, I mean I know you have to suffer for your art, but I'd prefer not to get expelled because somebody overheard us." Georgy added. "Whoops, sorry." Raff said sheepishly. Georgy continued telling his story and when he got to the part where he saw Philip get punched by the strange guy, Raff gave a low whistle. "Holy Cannoli." He said. "So you think it was that guy who... who did that to him?" "Sometimes I wonder how you manage to think and breathe at the same time.", Wally said mockingly. "Do you think Philip did it to himself?" Raff ignored him. "And now you think that scumbag Kevin is selling dope to Anna?" He asked. Georgy's eyebrows shot up. "You know her?" "Well, um, not exactly." Raff mumbled, suddenly flustered. "I mean, well, I just asked around a bit, you know, like one does and... happened to find out her name. She's in her last year here already, so I doubt she'd be interested in an eighth-grade loser like, I mean, that is..." He trailed off. "So you made a pass at her?" Wally asked. "What, no!" Raff said indignantly. "'Course not. I bet she doesn't look at anyone who isn't in high school yet." "Is she with someone?" Wally pressed on. "Uh, why do you care?" Georgy interrupted the exchange. Raff took a deep breath. "Well, listen here son, when a boy turns a certain age, he will notice some changes..." "Yeah, not like you – always, window-shopping and never stopping to buy." Wally said. "Can't afford anything on display." Georgy mumbled. "Shed your dowdy feathers and fly, a little bit." Raff went on in a sing-song voice. Georgy had to stop him before he started singing. "Very funny but I'm just saying what's the point of deluding yourself into believing you got a chance. She's way out of your league." "'Fraid your right about that, Georgy girl." Raff said and sighed. "But you know how it is." "Actually I don't. How is it?" Raff was suddenly blushing. "Well, you know, with the girls and the- Never mind." He mumbled. "You're all talk, aren't you?" Georgy said matter-of-factly. "Chasing after skirts like that is what cowards do, 'cause you now it won't happen in a million years." "Sure." Wally said in a dead-man voice. "Let's just pretend you dream of nothing at night." "Exactly right." Raff said with a grin and condescendingly patted his shoulder, when the bell rang.

During recess, the four of them were standing together in a corner of the schoolyard. They were supposed to be discussing the details of their plan, but Georgy found his attention straying toward Kevin and his little group of friends over and over again. "Just as I thought." He mumbled under his breath. "She just bought something again." There had obviously been an exchange between Kevin and the girl. It hadn't taken more than thirty seconds. He thought about it for a moment and turned to the others. "Let's tell Olly." He said matter-of -factly. "If we want to actually do something, we can't just be three people." "Yes, obviously we'll need to be at least four." Wally said, raising his eyebrows at Georgy. "You sure about this?" He asked in a more serious tone. "Um, s'cuse me?" Olly interjected. "Tell

34

me what exactly?" Georgy nodded, looked at Wally, looked at Raff and began to tell the story.

"Wow, that's nuts. ", Olly said when he had finished. "I mean, I get you can't go to the police. But you could maybe write an anonymous letter. Along the lines of: Hey, that Kevin-guy's a menace, maybe check his sock drawers or something." "Yeah, that might work." Georgy said. "But he probably doesn't hide his stash in his drawer, if he isn't entirely stupid. Plus, an anonymous letter doesn't really prove anything." "Yeah.", Wally agreed. "I bet they get a ton of those just as jokes from stupid kids who want to mess with their friends. Not likely they'd start an investigation over it." "You're probably right." Raff said. "So I guess we gotta take a more hands-on approach." "We'll need proof." "And where will you get it?" Olly asked wide-eyed. "Don't know yet. I guess we'll just have to watch them for now." They looked at each other in grim determination and Georgy nodded. "Can I get the girl? To survey, I mean." Olly asked hopefully. "How about you start by growing some hair on your chest." Raff said, grinning. "I'll take the girl, of course." Georgy rolled his eyes. "No, you won't." He said. "You'll absolutely blow it. Then you'll be the one hauled off to jail 'cause she probably thought you were stalking her." "Oh, what, chick-magnet that you are, gonna take over and show us how it's done." Raff grumbled. "You been hitting Kevin's stash or something?" Wally cut them off, sounding all business. "You seem to be hallucinating that this is some sort of dumb dating show. No, the three of us will take care of Kevin and Georg can watch Anna." Then a lazy grin split his face in half when he added: "Plus no-one's gonna suspect anything from our precious baby boy over
35

here." "Geez, thanks." Georgy said in mock-offense. "But let's get down to brass tacks."

Olly had taken it upon himself to unlatch the window in the men's restroom of the museum. His parents had announced to him that they were going to take a look at the exhibit that weekend and when he, in turn, had announced that he would simply love to tag along, his father had made this big deal of how Olly either had to be sick or aliens had replaced his son.

When the four of them met on the graveyard, just before the clock struck two in the morning, they had to admit it was a bit spooky, though none of them did it out loud. Instead, they stood there in their coats, gloves and scarfs, trying to put on brave faces over their chattering teeth. "So, did you do it?" Georgy asked, peering at Olly through the darkness. "'Course I did. What, do you think so little of me?" Olly snapped. He was obviously on edge, though it was probably because of the cold. There were only a few clouds veiling the sky, the light of the moon intermittently shining treacherously upon the graveyard. Hopefully nobody would come to pay their beloved departed an early morning visit. Georgy suppressed a shiver. The dark outline of the church tower was clearly visible against the blue grey of the night sky. Georgy didn't know how long he had been staring when he suddenly noticed Wally by his side. The other boy was looking up in silent rapture and when he said: "Let's go climb it." In a quiet voice, there weren't any objection.

The view was breathtaking. Georgy had read in the community newspaper that the tower was over 150 feet tall. Still, reading it and actually standing on it, being able to see for miles and miles into the distance were two entirely different things. Even the masts of the USCGC Eagle, nicknamed America's tall ship, were only a bit taller. Up there, on the church tower, he could pretend he was standing between the halyards, taking down the sails. He closed his eyes, his hands hovering a finger's breadth above the railing, listening to the wind whipping past his ears...

Walter giving a low whistle shook him from his reverie. He and Ralf had his hands buried deep within their pockets, both of them surveying the scenery. "Look at how far you can see." Wally said quietly. "Over there, the city. It's gorgeous, isn't it?" What would usually have been followed by jeering and snide remarks was followed only by awed silence. When they came across the gaping hole in the wall that had not too long ago housed the church's clock, on their decent down the scaffolding the boys decided that they would climb in there sometime soon as well, to look around the clock tower.

First, it was time to move some furniture. In reality, it was pretty easy. It took them about one and a half hours to carry the benches into the museum and the sofas onto the graveyard, after a bit of initial difficulty hoisting the first couch up to the window and some bruised fingers.

Once they were done, they spent some time sitting on one of the plush eyesores, imagining the looks on people's faces when they came across them.

And it hit like a bomb. The pastor spent at least two services ranting from the pulpit, the mayor threw a fit and the community workers who had been tasked with bringing everything back to where it belonged could be heard complaining all the way through.

On Monday morning Raff came dashing into the classroom almost bursting with barely reigned in laughter and immediately launched into a theatrical impersonation of his aunt July, who had been over for coffee that Sunday.

"Oh, dear, you positively must accompany me to the graveyard some time – love what they have done to the place, those new benches are simply darling. I wasn't even aware that the community was so well off, but it is good to see those taxpayer dollars at work. God bless this country."

Chapter 3   Old F's new sorrows

It took quite a while for the confusion surrounding the couch incident to die down. Pastor Flick, even though there was no reason to believe, let alone any concrete evidence that they had been involved at all, kept ranting at his students during confirmation class.

Georgy and Raff had been born in the same year and as such would receive their confirmation together. Wally as well, in a sense, though his parents' church was one town over. "Do you have any plans what you're going to do with the money you'll get for going through with this?" Raff asked, lying on his back on a table while they were waiting for the Pastor in the community center. "I asked my parents to take me to Boston. I wanna take a look around the USS Constitution." "You and your ridiculous ship-obsession." Raff mumbled, shaking his head. "Don't worry." Georgy said. "I don't expect you to understand."
"Good, 'cause I don't." "I'm going to be sailing the seas someday, so I care about stuff like that." Georgy said with a shrug. "Yeah, yeah, I get it." Raff countered with a snort. "I wanted to become a conductor when I was a kid." Georgy didn't take the bait. "That's different." He said. "Two more years and I'll be gone." "Whatever you say. As for me, I will be using the money to buy myself a scooter. I'll be 16 come June. Might even make me too cool to hang around you losers."

Just that moment, a small commotion broke out in the far corner of the room. A few boys, led by none other than Kevin, had begun taking their songbooks out of their boxes and stacking them in front of the door. One of them appeared to have overestimated his carrying capacity and with a curse and a crash what he had been holding in his hands a moment prior was suddenly lying all over the floor. "What are you doing?" Urs, a pretty girl with brown curly hair asked. "Shut up, watch and learn." Kevin said snootily. "Who died and made you boss?" Urs shot back. "I said can it, twerp!"

The boys continued layering book upon book until the resulting construct almost spanned the distance from floor to door handle. The last book had to be forcefully jammed in there. Now the door would no longer open. Georgy quietly wondered whether he should congratulate Kevin on his ingenuity but decided that he was quite content with the current placement of his organs inside of his body. He was traditional that way. "What d'you do that for?" Raff asked. "Gee, Ralfy, you're even dumber than you look.", Kevin said derisively. "If the preacher man can't get in here, he can't start his boring classes. It's brilliant, really." "No kidding." Raff hissed, shifting on his table. Georgy could see that his neck and ears had turned a vibrant shade of red. "Well, if you hate it so much, what are you doing here in the first place?" Urs asked irately, glaring at the stack of books. "More importantly..." Georgy said quietly. "You do realize we're stuck in here now, right?"

Somebody tried to push down the door handle. When it caught on the books, the person on the other side began banging on the door. "Open up, you darned brats." The pastor hollered. "Sorry but we can't." Said a girl from Kevin's gang. "Our lord and savior Jesus Christ has decided that this door shall remain shut." For a moment the pastor said nothing, likely standing on the other side in stunned silence, then: "That's- Open this door at once!" "Our Lord Jesus Christ made this door impassable with holy means! Would you defy the word of our savior?" The girl asked. "How dare- Wait until your parents hear of this! When I get my hands-!" "You need Jesus!" The girl screamed back when Georgy pushed past her. "Let's just open it." He said quietly. "You think he'll trying to run down the door?" Urs asked, just as quietly. "Let's not risk it." Mumbled Raff, glaring at Kevin. Nobody tried to stop them when they pushed the stack of books to the side.

The door swung open with a bang, colliding painfully with Georgy's shoulder and knocking down the books in the process. Raff and Urs, with expressions of shock on their faces had managed to jump back in time and were staring at Georgy, hunched over, one hand clasping his shoulder and the pastor, who looked about ready to do something of a very unholy nature. His face a terrifying shade of purple, he was stalking toward Georgy. "Of course - but of course! - It was you." He growled.   "But he only tried- " "Quiet!" The pastor hissed at Urs, who'd likely meant to say something helpful. Georgy knew that Kevin and his gang would never admit that it had been their stupid excuse of a joke. And why should they? Somebody else getting blamed for their dumb pranks likely made them even more worthwhile. "This will have consequences!" Pastor Flick said, jabbing at his shoulder   with   his   finger.   "Actual consequences!" Nobody said anything. The pastor gave a huff, deflated a little and went to the front of

41

the room. "Come see me after class, George." He called over his shoulder. "And now clean up this mess!"

Class went by in a monotonous blur. The pastor spoke and the kids listened. Georgy was quietly fuming. He was mad at everyone. Mad at Kevin for being a colossal jerk wad, at the others for not getting their stupid mouths open to defend him, at himself for just taking it like a wuss and at the stupid pastor for not even giving him a chance to explain himself. He knew that Raff was giving him sidelong glances from time to time, but he ignored it. By the end of the lesson he'd tell Mister Flick what had really happened, he decided. He wasn't going to take the fall for someone like Kevin, let alone for something so utterly and ridiculously uncreative. After everyone had said their goodbyes and he was just about to purposefully walk up to the pastor's table, not even looking at Raff, who was awkwardly standing by the door, Kevin caught his arm. "You better not rat." He hissed. "You better keep your smart mouth shut." The he walked out the room like nobody's business.

"What do you have to say in your defense?" The pastor asked, the last word punctuated by the sound of his briefcase snapping shut. Georgy really wanted to say something, anything at all but in the face of the pastors anger he seemed to have forgotten how words worked. Instead, he avoided the man's eyes and stared at the floor. He wouldn't believe me anyway, he thought miserably, and this day's already been bad enough without Kevin and his gang re-arranging my insides for snitching. "Cat's got your tongue?" The pastor asked, swinging his briefcase of the table. "Let

42

me give you an incentive then." The man shrugged on his coat and tied his scarf before continuing to speak, giving Georgy ample opportunity to change his mind. When he didn't he gave a huff and said: "You'll scour the church floors after every service. That means not just on Sundays, do you understand?" Georgy nodded and could have kicked himself. "And you better make sure your record stays clean from now on. If news gets to me that you've been messing around again, I'll write to your father." The pastor inhaled deeply, seemed to consider for a moment and nodded. "Carry this to my car." He said, unceremoniously flinging his briefcase at Georgy, before walking out of the door. "Move it along." He called from the hallway. " I don't have all day." Georgy nodded again, grinding his teeth and his nails digging into his palms as they left the community center.

Everything sucked. No one appreciated him at home, his parents may even have been happier had it just been his brother there. He didn't have a girlfriend, though not because he didn't want one like his friends kept saying. He didn't do great at school and though he didn't care about the grades, he felt like the other students didn't care about *him* and that was the problem. And now this. He was angry and embarrassed to the extent that he didn't know what to do with himself. He wanted to scream and cry and possibly vanish away into the ground all at the same time.

When he got to the pastor's car, the feeling had past to an extent. The lock on the right front door was busted, so he didn't need a key.

He was already making his way home across the graveyard, dragging his feet along the gravel when the pastor called back to him from the sacristy. Georgy briefly considered to just continuous walking but ultimately decided against it. Wordlessly, the pastor handed him a steel-bladed scraper from above. "How about you go get a head-start on your work?" He asked, not really expecting a reply. "There are wax drippings all around the altar. Get rid of them and you can leave." Without another word, the man turned on his heel and vanished into the church. For a few seconds Georgy just stood there, angrily glaring up to the window but he couldn't very well risk pretending that he hadn't heard now. Glumly, he went into the church.

In front of the altar were a few puddles of congealed wax, a by-product of the candles burning throughout the service.

Georgy knelt down and began scraping away. It was frustrating work, the wax being so smooth that it was hard to find purchase on it. He looked up and his gaze landed on the crucified Jesus above him, who was looking down from deep-set mournful eyes. At least Georgy wasn't suffering by himself. So much for divine justice, he thought, the scraper sliding off the ' wax yet again, leaving barely a mark on it. 'I'm crawling around on my knees while the others are having themselves a grand old time at home.'. He looked up at the cross yet again and noticed that something was off.

In the time before Christmas in the previous year, they had decorated the interior of the church like they always did with Christmas trees and hanging lights. That year's decoration crew had been especially clumsy, it seemed, and someone had broken off a large piece of crucified Jesus' halo. If you looked closely and from where Georgy was huddled on the floor, it looked like he had grown two tiny horns. Georgy couldn't help but smile. That explains it, he thought to himself. But to leave the poor guy like that. What was the pastor thinking? An idea began forming in his head.

A few hours later, Georgy was walking toward Mister Flick's car again. It was two thirty in the morning; his dad had spent hours in the living room, watching a rerun of some boxing match that had been advertised what had felt like weeks. 'George Foreman vs. Jimmy Young, the 17th of March, don't miss it.' Or something to that effect, anyway.

He quietly opened the door. This time, he'd be taking something out rather than putting something in. Armed with a set of socket spanners from his father's workshop, he lay on the driver's seat coming face to face with the steering wheel. With a screw-driver serving as a make-shift lever, he managed to pry the emblem loose in a matter of seconds, revealing the bolts underneath. It took him a while to figure out the correct bit size but once he had, the wheel came off in under five minutes and he stealthily exited the car.

Sneaking across the graveyard, he recovered the backpack, which he had deposited between some bushes only a few hours earlier. He unzipped it and took out a wadded-up newspaper and a can of spray-paint. Unfolding the paper in the light of a streetlamp, next to one of the benches he had just recently been lugging around town, he placed the wheel on it and uncapped the paint. 'Fast-drying', it said on the can. It was another item he had 'borrowed' from his dad's workshop, without asking, of course. After about 20 minutes the paint had dried enough for him to pick up the wheel without turning his hands golden. He quickly stuffed everything back into his backpack and began his ascent up the scaffolding of the church tower. Going in through the front gate would have been far more comfortable but they'd started locking the church as of late. Not that he minded much. Georgy got to the hole in the tower where the clock had been and climbed in. The darkness on the inside seemed all encompassing, so he had no choice but to take out his flashlight.

The horned statue of Jesus was looking down at him. Ever since confirmation classes had started and Georgy had become more of a regular at church, he had learned a thing or two about the place. He got a table from the sacristy, placed it underneath the cross and lifted a chair on top of it. Once he had climbed on, the chair and table seeming to buckle under his weight, he stood up on his toes and reached for what was left of the halo. He couldn't help but feel a little guilty, when his hands closed around it. "Uh, sorry, um... Sir." he mumbled and cringed. No, that didn't make it better in the slightest. Maybe he just shouldn't say anything at all. The wood gave way with a snap that echoed off the church walls and made Georgy freeze for a moment before he remembered that it was the middle of the night and the place was locked. Releasing a breath he hadn't realized he had been holding, he began rummaging through his backpack, pulling out a hammer and a few nails he haphazardly trapped between his teeth. Slowly, a little reluctant, he positioned one of them against the back of the Jesus statue's head. "I'm just trying to fix you, I swear." He mumbled through his teeth as he began driving it in. The cross, which was held in place by two metal wires, was swaying dangerously from front to back as though in protest. Georgy resolved not to think about it and just finish the job, pushing away the feeling of dread that had settled in his gut. When he was done, he bent down, plucked the golden steering wheel from between his legs and stuck it on there without looking.

Once he had put everything back where it belonged, remainder of the halo excluded, he was either going to keep it as a trophy or get rid of it as soon as possible, he hadn't decided yet, he stood in front of the altar and shone his flashlight at the cross. Maybe his mind was playing tricks on him but with his halo restored, Jesus seemed to look a little less tortured.

The next morning came with a vengeance. Georgy barely managed to drag himself out of bed and honestly considered pretending to be sick, even though it came with a slew of annoying side-effects, like his mom recruiting the old neighbor lady, who seemed to delight in barging into his room every other hour or so to check on him. It was the sudden thought of that pungent cabbage stew of hers that motivated him to pull himself together and go to school anyway.

He had just made it to the classroom, already having resigned himself to a day of exhausted semi-consciousness, when something unexpected happened. One moment he was about to close the

47

door behind himself, the next he was flinching away from a flurry of brown and beige that came barreling toward him, only to suddenly be standing toe to toe with Urs. "Uh, can I help you?" He asked awkwardly while she motioned for two other girls to come closer. Georgy was sure that he had seen them somewhere before. "I'm just really sorry for yesterday." Urs said and one of her friends nodded enthusiastically. Suddenly, it dawned on Georgy that he knew them from confirmation class. Very briefly, he tried to remember their names, when he suddenly felt Urs' hand on his lower arm and was forced to abort all coherent thought in favor of fighting off a blush. "That was real low of me." Urs went on. "But you see, Mister Flick's real scary when he's mad and..." She sighed and shook her head. "No, that's a lame excuse. I'm just really sorry, okay? Was it bad? Did you get in trouble? Mister Flick isn't going to write to your parents, is he?" Gradually, the confusion Georgy had felt only seconds prior morphed into pride. "T'was nothing." He mumbled, trying to square his shoulders without Urs noticing. "I mean, it's fine as long as you guys didn't get in trouble. Over kids' stuff like that." He regretted the words almost as soon as they left his mouth. Kid's stuff. What a stupid thing to say. Now Urs would think he was arrogant. Urs looked impressed, though not entirely convinced but Georgy was too busy mentally berating himself to notice, when Miss Sanders entered the room.

"Good morning, class." Mrs. Sanders said, far too cheerfully. "Good morning, Mrs. Sanders.", came the far less enthusiastic reply. Miss Sanders either didn't notice or chose to ignore it. Still smiling brightly, she put her bag on the table. "I hope you remembered to bring the books I passed out last time. I know "The

Sorrows of young Werther" aren't exactly required reading but seeing how we are ahead of schedule, a little foray into foreign literature couldn't hurt. And what better time for it than now that the literature club is done with it? Plus, we can only stomach so many mocking birds and midsummer night's dreams, can't we?" A few of the student's murmured in half-hearted agreement. Mrs. Sanders was a nice lady and calling her out on her stupid ideas was like kicking a puppy, so they mostly limited themselves to exchanging annoyed looks. Raff unceremoniously dumped his copy on his desk, obviously trying to make some sort of non-verbal statement but Georgy didn't notice. When he closed his eyes, it was like he could still feel Urs' hand on his arm.

During recess Wally, Raff and he stood in their usual corner on the schoolyard. "Man, I thought I was going to fall asleep when she began reading from that thing." Wally said with a sigh. "Hard to believe people used to speak like that. Non-ironically, I mean." "Who cares." Georgy mumbled numbly. The touched-by-girl high had only carried him through about half of the lesson. "I hope he doesn't just spend the entire book crying about how pretty the fireflies are." "Guess people didn't have anything better to do before comics and big screens." Wally said, shrugging, then he turned to Raff who was staring off to the side. "Is the world about to end or do you actually not have an opinion on something for once?" Raff countered with a shrug of his own "Well, I honestly don't care. And besides, aren't there more important things to talk about? Like, did we find out anything new about our little gang of dealers?" "I think Kevin stashes the stuff in the shed on his dad's garden plot.", Wally said. "I followed him a couple times after school last week and he seems to go there an awful lot. Gets in, gets out – real suspicious, if you ask me. He also seems to have about 16 buyers, though I can't say for sure. You guys find anything interesting?" "Nope, nothing." Raff said. "I don't think his little friends have anything to do with it." "Georgy?" His friends were looking at him expectantly. "Yeah, chick-magnet like yourself should have had it easy." Raff said quirking a brow. "Did you see Urs fawning over him earlier? Real cute, wasn't it?" Georgy made a face. "You're just jealous.", He said, without meaning it. "Yeah, yeah. That was an arm-rub to behold." Wally cut in, before Raff had the chance to respond. "I'm sure Raff will dream of it, or something. But did you find anything?" "Well..."

"I just know that her name is Anna Dasher. She's in her last year here and lives up on the mountain in a huge mansion." "Great, so you got nothing." Raff said dryly. "Geez, Raff. Don't recall you finding out anything useful." Georgy shot back. "That's 'cause I got stuck with a bad lead." Raff grumbled indignantly, pointing a finger at Georgy. "Because you insisted you get the girl. Had I been the one to follow her..." "You'd be sitting in a cell right now, as we've already established." Wally joined in again, grinning at them both. Raff visibly deflated. "It's harder than it looks." Georgy said without much humor. "I don't know how to get close to her without it being creepy." "Yeah, we get that." Wally said. "Is there anything else?" "Not much. Her mom's a model, her dad's an architect. Quite famous, too. He does mostly mansions, malls... that kind of thing. Anyway, the point is they have a lot of money." "Are you sure *that*'s all you found out?" Raff asked sullenly. "Well, not entirely but almost. She gets something from Kevin about once per week, her mom drops her off at school every morning, in one of those big fancy cars and she's got supply duty this week, same as I." "Okay." Wally said, pensively chewing on the inside of his cheek. "So, what's our plan of attack?" Georgy gave a shrug. "Watch and wait, I guess. Maybe we can find out where Kevin gets the stuff or something." "Probably the only thing we can do." Raff rejoined. He turned to Wally and smiled. "Hope you get some nice views of Kevin when you follow him around." "Don't worry." Wally said, without missing a beat. "I'll take some pictures for your collection."

As the day progressed, the news of someone stealing the pastor's steering wheel spread like wild fire. "Hey, you hear the latest?" Raff asked Georgy a few hours later. "Sure did." Georgy said curtly. He swore he saw a look of suspicion flit across Raff's face. He could barely reign in a grin. "So..." Raff went on, obviously trying very hard to only sound mildly interested and failing miserably. "You wouldn't happen to know anything about that, would you?" "Would you like to know where it went?" "You're pulling my leg, it was you?! I knew it! Geez, man, innocent little Georgy. Just be careful they don't catch you. Man, that's so awesome!" Georgy patiently waited for Raff to finish, then he said with a grin: "Next Sunday, during the service, just look up at our savior on the cross." Raff stared at him in slack-jawed awe.

"It's pay-back time for our dear pastor now, isn't it?" Raff asked when he had regained control of his face. "You got it." Georgy said solemnly. "The sorrows of young Werther now are the sorrows old Flick." They looked at each other and broke into laughter. "So, what's next?" Raff wondered aloud. "Don't know yet." Georgy said. "But I'm sure I'll think of something."

The last lesson for the day had been Geography. Georgy, on supply duty, had been tasked with returning the map, they had used in class to the supply room. It housed a great variety of maps, books and items of educational interest, like a skeleton, which's authenticity, became a hotly debated topic whenever a teacher decided to bust it out and a few taxidermies bugs and animals. The halls were deserted; everybody was already on their way home or hidden away in some clubroom or other. When he was about to round the corner to the supply room, Georgy heard a strange noise. It sounded like someone was crying or maybe cursing. Suddenly curious, he peered around the corner.

His surprise must have been written on his face. It was Anna Dasher, tinkering with the lock. "What're you looking at?!", She hissed when she noticed him staring. Georgy was stunned silent for a moment. Was this girl really taking to him? "Oh, whoops, um, sorry. Is, uh, something the matter?" He asked lamely. The girl's head whipped around, executing an impressive hair-flip in the process, as she gave him a good, long glare. "Forgot to take the key out of the lock again, frickin' moron that I am." "Uh, what d'you mean 'Again'?" He stuttered, trying to seem natural. "Again! Again, like it happened before, what do you think?!", she almost screamed, giving the door a hard shove and then a kick for good measure. Georgy had never switched from being incredibly embarrassed to being incredibly intimidated in that short a span of time and took half a step back before he could stop himself. Trying to keep the conversation

52

going to distract her, he scrambled for something to say. "But... there's no key in the lock." He supplied helpfully. The girl took a deep breath. It sounded a bit like a burning fuse. "That's because it's on the inside." She said seethingly. "Oh." Said Georgy. 'Wow.' He thought. 'I'm a moron.' But he couldn't let that stop him, he would probably never get a chance to talk to this girl again. "Hey, I've got a key right here.", He said, aiming for cool and landing on voice-change. Minor setback, he thought. "I'll just unlock the door for you." Her face relaxed a little and Georgy couldn't help blushing a bit. 'She's even prettier when she isn't about to tear your head off.' He noted absently. "That's all nice and good, but that won't work. You can only unlock the door if there isn't already a key stuck in it." "Oh, now I get it." Georgy mumbled, staring at Anna, bug-eyed. She seemed to have forgotten about him already. Rapping her knuckles across the wood, she broke into another stream of curses. "What's the point of that new security lock, if it comes at the cost of the door handles? You think someone's gonna try stealing some dumb, stuffed rat or something? Get real!" "Yeah, I know." Georgy said. "You always need the key to open the door from either side now." "Exactly. I left the key in the lock and that thing...", she pointed at the automatic closing mechanism atop the door. "Pulled it shut." "And it's the second time this happened to you? I don't get how you'd manage that at all, let alone twice in a row." Georgy said disbelievingly, before he managed to stop himself. To his surprise, the girl didn't immediately jump down his throat but buried her head in her hands. "Yes! Honestly, you'd think I'd wise up after the first time. My mom's gonna kill me, if the school sends her another bill. Last time the

53

janitor had to get a locksmith to bust the thing open. It was super expensive." Georgy was just about to tell her that her family could probably afford it but that time he thought better of it. Instead, he said: "No worries, you'll get your key back tomorrow. I'll find a way." Did he have a plan? No. But how many more chances like that would he get? "Oh, yeah?" Anna raised a brow at him and sized him up. George felt strangely exposed. "You know that you can't just force it open, right? I need that key back or I'll get in trouble. Don't, like, give me yours to play hero or something like that." "Don't worry, I'll take care of everything." Georgy said with a confidence he didn't feel. No turning back now. Anna snorted and shook her head. "Sure, Mister bigshot." She said. "Let's see what you can do." "I'll get you your key..." Georgy began, somewhat hesitantly, "In exchange for a favor." If he could just get her to tell him something about Kevin and his gang. Maybe find out where he got his stuff or track down someone who knew. Anna snorted again. "Of course. Whatever. Pull this off and I'll even take you out to dinner or something." That took him by surprise and he blushed furiously. "Really?" he blurted. "If you would... that would be nice." When he noticed the semi-sympathetic look that had replaced the sneer on Anna's face, he suddenly felt like an idiot again. "Listen..." She said looking over her shoulder, obviously eager for the conversation to end. "I really need to get going. My mom's probably already waiting for me." "Okay." Georgy mumbled. "Um... See you tomorrow?" She had already walked halfway down the corridor when he'd worked up the nerve to call after her. "Hey, once I got the key, how can I get it to you?" "Meet me in front of the chemistry lab during recess or before school starts." She called back, without breaking stride. "A-alright then." Georgy said and it felt like he was talking to himself. Nobody else was listening.

He looked around. The halls were still empty. He quickly inspected the lock – it wasn't anything special but it wouldn't be easy to pick either. Pulling out his key he tried to unlock the door, but it didn't budge. Georgy sighed. He quickly needed to come up with something – either that or steer clear of Anna for a while. The fact that she would graduate in a few months wasn't much of a consolation.

Just then, he remembered the talk he'd had with Raff and Wally earlier, the way Raff had teased him, and suddenly he was all the more determined to see it through. Not to mention, he didn't want to make a liar of himself after how he'd acted in front of Anna. Even if she had been incredibly rude to him. 'Strange', he thought, 'Aren't potheads supposed to be mellow?' After stashing the map he'd been carrying in an empty classroom, he got on his way to the Woodman residence.

The Woodmans lived in the official lodgings provided to the janitor by the school, above the bandstand. Wally's mother opened the door, called for her son and Wally and Georgy went to Wally's room, where Georgy quickly relayed what happened. "She's going to take you out to eat if you get her key back? Jeez, it's your lucky day, isn't it?" Wally said, smiling wryly. "Well, at least I think so." Georgy replied, sitting on Wally's desk. "I mean, I don't think *she* thinks I can do it, so maybe she was just saying it..." He fell silent and shook his head in frustration. "Not that it matters! There's no way I'll get that thing back. If I break the lock, I break the key. Then she'll get in even more trouble and I'll be lucky if she doesn't kill me." "It's worth giving a shot." Wally said, hopping up from where he sat on the bed. "Wouldn't want you to end up an old spinster. Just give me a sec." "I'm not so sure. You shoulda seen what she did to that door. Real violent." Georgy said in exasperation but Wally had already left the room. He returned a moment later, triumphantly extending his hand toward George. In his open palm lay a key. "What's that?" Georgy asked, though he could already guess. "It's a spare." Wally responded, grinning. "My dad has six or seven of them, in case someone loses one. Take it and give it to her. Tell her to return that one." Wally smiled, genuinely for once as Georgy stared at him, speechless. "I owe you one." He said, once he had remembered how to speak.

"Yeah, you do. Especially because if you just give her the key people are gonna catch on that something's wrong. Nobody'll be able to get into the supply room and if all the keys are accounted for, the entire thing could fall back on me." Georgy considered for a moment, then he gave Wally a pat on the shoulder. "Got it covered." He said. "If they find that the lock has been broken in from the outside tomorrow, nobody'll think twice of it. Some evildoer'll just break in there tonight, if you catch my drift. The key in there will vanish – it probably won't survive anyway." "So much for avoiding collateral damage with your pranks." Wally mumbled, amused. "True." Said Georgy. "But the lock will have to be broken one way or another, doesn't really matter if by my hands or some locksmiths." "No, actually..." Wally mused. "The school's gonna save some money 'cause the only thing that'll have to be bought will be a new lock. Not to mention, classes won't be delayed because everyone will be able to get the supplies they need." "Yeah, imagine how sad everyone would be if class didn't start on time." Georgy said, raising his eyebrows. Wally gave a snort.

Executing the plan hadn't been any trouble at all. Georgy borrowed a drill and an extension cord from his dad's workshop, which were usually only taken out of the closet when his dad had to work on stainless steel or something like that. Really handy, having access to all that stuff, Georgy thought as he snuck out the door.

As per usual, he climbed through the window of the boy's restroom. Wally had taken another trip to school and unlatched it for him a few hours prior, having easy access to school keys and all that. Silently, Georgy thanked whatever entity had decreed he should have a friend and wingman like Wally.

The drill had made short work of the lock. His mom had broken a key in their front door once and his dad had, cursing like Georgy had never heard anyone curse before, fixed the problem in a matter of minutes. Using 10milimeter drill bit, he drilled a hole at exactly the point where one would usual put the key. It was important to make sure the rotation count remain low, so the drill wouldn't overheat, his dad had said. It took about 10 minutes, then he could use a broad screwdriver to push the tumblers out of the way and unlock the door.

He had sacrificed his very own teddy bear for this, not that he would have admitted to still having one in the first place, but he had to disguise the break-in somehow and some stupid student's prank was as good an option as any. *Make stuffed animals not taxidermies, protesting for the rights of my fleshy brethren,* he had written on a piece of cardboard, which now hung from the teddy's neck. He placed it between the taxidermied animals, picked up the fragments of Anna's key, which had fallen to the floor and put them in his pocket.

One hour later he was lying in bed, comfortable beneath the covers, rolling what was left of the key between his fingers. He spent a good long while imagining how Anna would react once he gave her back the key. The longer he kept it going, the crazier these imaginings became until, just before falling asleep he saw Anna and himself sitting on a porch on matching rocking chairs, watching over their grandchildren.

The next morning, Georgy put on a fresh pair of jeans and a matching dress shirt. Inspecting himself in the mirror, he came to the conclusion that it would likely look better if he finally bulked up a bit (which was probably going to happen any day now. He wouldn't stay skinny forever. Right?) He washed and brushed his hair and even tried shining his shoes before deciding that just impressing Anna with his actions would probably be more effective. They had breakfast in relative silence, Georgy almost too nervous to eat his toast. "Why's Georgy smell like da'?" his little brother suddenly piped up. Georgy gave him the most venomous look he could muster. "Rat." He muttered under his breath, but it was already too late. His mother had just come into the room, smiling widely in a way that was almost unerring and lent over to take a whiff. "And when're you gonna introduce yer girlfriend to us, eh darlin'?" "Er, w-what?" Georgy stuttered. . His mother's smile grew impossibly wider as she tapped her nose. "Yer father's cologne yer usin'." "Oh, that's, uh, that's nothing." Georgy stammered, blindly reaching for his schoolbag. "Just, uh, I just haven't showered in a while, is all." "That so?" His mother asked, clearly amused. "Well, gotta go." Georgy mumbled, before he beat a hasty retreat to avoid more questions. "You got at least ten more minutes!" His mother hollered after him but Georgy was already out the door.

Combing his hair had been absolutely useless. After racing to school on his bike, he looked like he had been tossed around by a tornado. Only when he had started breaking a sweat had he slowed down a bit, so getting up early hadn't been entirely in vain.

A few minutes later, he was standing around the hallway in front of the chemistry lab, his face hot and unflatteringly red. His hair was mussed and sweat beaded his forehead in a way that could not possibly have been attractive. Chewing on his tongue, tightly clutching the key in his hand for support, he was waiting for Anna. A stream of students that didn't seem to want to end passed him by, none of them paying him any mind, talking to their friends or rushing to their lockers. He kept checking his watch and could barely believe that he had only been standing there for ten minutes, when she finally showed, surrounded by a flock of other girls who were eyeing him curiously when he motioned her over. She didn't even notice him at first, until one of her friends pointed at him and whispered something he couldn't understand. A few of the girls laughed. Anna tilted her head and looked at him imploringly. When he quietly nodded his head, she broke away from her friends and held out a hand toward him. Without even the slightest trace of hesitation, Georgy dropped the key onto her palm, trying for a confident smile. "Thanks." She whispered, then turned and vanished in the chemistry lab. Georgy slowly let his hand sink from where it hovered awkwardly in mid-air, staring at the door as it closed in his face. He felt like an idiot.

"So, how'd it go? She gonna wine and dine you or what?" Even though Georgy had done his best to avoid his friends since that morning, Wally and Raff had somehow managed to corner him during recess. "Dunno." He mumbled, glumly staring at the ground. "What happened?" Wally asked. Georgy suppressed a sigh and told the two of them what had happened the night before and how everything had worked out great until his luck had decided to change overnight. Raff, who hadn't been aware of the plan, kept shaking his head all the way through. "I hope you're still picking your moment and didn't just run to her when you first got the chance, like some lost puppy." He said, eyeing Georgy curiously. Georgy swallowed and said nothing. "You blew it." Wally stated matter-of-factly. Raff shook his head again, though for different reasons this time. "Oh, boy." He mumbled. "You got so much to learn." "What's that supposed to mean?" Georgy growled. He could feel his face turn red. "Nothing." Raff said with a shrug. "I'm sure you'll be the best of friends in no time. Maybe you'll even get to be maid of honor at her wedding." "Whatever." Georgy shot back defensively. "I think she just didn't have time or something. She took the key and went to class. So..." Wally and Raff exchanged meaningful glances. "Sure." Wally said, clasping a hand over Georgy's shoulder. "Hey, don't sweat it. She may be back later." And after a moment's hesitation he added: "And even if she isn't, there are more fish in the sea, right?"

"How'd the chemistry test treat you?", Raff asked during recess. "Solid B." Wally said with an easy smile. "You?" "D-." Raff said with a grin of his own. "Still a pass. And I figure the C- from the first one should cancel that out." "You sure that's how that works?" Wally asked, grinning. "Whatever man, still a pass. Hey, look who finally decided to show up." Georgy, who had been listening as he approached, rolled his eyes. "Had some business to take care of." Raff chuckled. "What, you do so poorly on that test that it made you sick?" "Your face makes me sick." Georgy mumbled. "Harsh!" Raff slapped his hand over his heart and threw his head back dramatically. "Seriously though, how'd you do?" Georgy suppressed a sigh and decided to bite the bullet. "A-" He said so quickly, that for a second it seemed like the other hadn't understood him. "Really now?" Wally asked, quirking a brow while Raff stared at him in disbelief. "Yeah, wonders never cease." Georgy mumbled. "Listen, it's no big deal, I just..." "You a nerd or something?" A girl asked. The three of them shot around suddenly face to face with Anna. She was looking straight at George and, even more than that, she was smiling. "You got a minute?" "Make us proud." Wally whispered and gave Georgy a shove.

"Thanks again for the key thing. That was real nice of you." Anna said, once they had gotten some distance between themselves and Georgy's friends. Georgy was wordlessly trailing beside her. He had thought of so many cool things to say the night before but somehow couldn't remember any of them. "So how did you do it?" Anna asked, stopping abruptly. "I mean, there is a huge hole in the lock but somehow the key is fine." "Uhm, well, uh... Trade secret?" Georgy croaked, avoiding her eyes. Why did his voice always have to do that when he talked to this girl? Anna made a face, one hand on her hip and gave him a once-over. "You're not secretly Superman, are you? Melting through the lock with laser vision and then turning back time?" "Can only do that in places that don't have fire alarms." Georgy mumbled under his breath. To his surprise, Anna actually laughed at that. It must have been the most beautiful laugh he had ever heard. "C'mon, don't be like that! At least tell me if you put the Teddy there." "Well, I had disguised the break-in somehow, right?" "Right, so how's the key not   broken."
"That's   gotta   stay   secret,   you   know?"
"Oh, a secret, sure, I get it." Anna said, smiling. "You the secretive sort then? Anything worth knowing about?"
"Maybe." Georgy mumbled and shyly smiled back at her. When her smile widened, however, he quickly averted his eyes. "So, you're more like the Riddler." She stated amusement clearly audible in her voice. "Maybe." Georgy said again. "That's Batman, though." Anna shrugged. "So? I like Batman better anyway. Superman doesn't have to work for his

powers." "Bruce Wayne doesn't have to work for his money." Georgy responded. Anna considered for a moment. "True." She said, biting her lip. "But he has to rely on his wits. Being clever isn't something you can buy." Georgy didn't say anything. Was he really having a conversation about superheroes with the most popular girl at school? "What's your name, anyway? Should at least know the name of the man I'll cook dinner for." "C-cook dinner? As in... At your place?" George stuttered. "Yeah. Unless you want to break into a restaurant, so I can cook there. Oh. Or don't you want to-?" "No, no!" Georgy interrupted, "I mean yes! That would be-" he cleared his throat. "That would be nice." He took a deep breath. "George, my name's George." "Anna Dahser." Said Anna. "Okay." Georgy mumbled, staring at her as though she were an apparition. "Something on my face?" She asked. "No, no nothing." Georgy blurted, shaking his head for emphasis. "So, uh, when would be convenient for you. Having dinner, I mean." Anna tilted her head to the side and brushed her thumb over her lips. "How about Saturday?" Georgy felt like his stomach was dissolving. In a good way. "Sure." He said. "And maybe, just maybe." Anna said with a glint in her eyes. "You will tell me one or two of your secrets?" Georgy bashfully looked at the floor. "Just maybe." He muttered. "Good enough for me." Anna said, grinning. "Anyway, see you Saturday? Say, around seven?" Georgy nodded. Maybe his luck hadn't turned after all.

Chapter 4   Wrong on all accounts

"You're messing with me. You really got a date with her on Saturday?" When school was finally over, the three of them were slowly walking toward the bus stop and bike-stands. "I'll make you a deal." Raff said, grinning. "We switch. I'll just go in your stead and tell her it was really me who broke open the lock. Take it or leave it." "What, are you nuts?" Georgy laughed and punched Raff in the arm. "No deal!" "But I'm just so much more charming than you are." Raff went on. "And a great deal less clever." Wally said dryly. "I'm pretty sure Anna would catch on." "Speaking of clever." Raff said, furrowing his brows. "How on god's green earth did you manage an A on that test." "A-." Georgy corrected. "Whatever." Raff said with a shrug. "It all looks the same up there from where I am standing." Georgy looked away and waved dismissively. "I guess I just thought the topic was interesting." "Did you hit your head?" Raff laughed. "What's interesting about chemical oxidation?" "Well, look at it this way: It's the basis for everything that smells and goes boom. Who knows what that stuff could be used for. I already pocketed some kalium-nitrate and sulfur." "Are you building a stink bomb? You're not going to impress Anna with that." Said Raff. "Of course, not." Georgy said, rolling his eyes. His friends could be so uncreative sometimes.

The afternoon brought little good. It rained cats and dogs and pastor Flick was in a terrible mood. His steering wheel had still not been found and he had had to buy a new one to be able to continue using his car. Everybody tried to look as innocent as possible and not at all like the ordeal was the funniest thing they had ever heard of. The pastor as the proverbial shepherd was developing a decided dislike for his sheep. "I would like to remind you that stealing property of the church constitutes an act of sacrilege that our lord and savior will not look kindly upon when judgment day comes." "He should be the first to get punished, then." Georgy whispered to Raff. "I've seen him dip into the altar wine."

"Is there something you would like to share with us?" The pastor spun around so quickly that the wind created by the cassock swiped a few sheets of paper off their desks. "George, Ralf, why don't you indulge us." Something in the air seemed to shift when the man approached them. "No?" He asked. "Well, then perhaps you would like to contribute in another way. A valuable service to the community, so to speak. The baptismal font needs to be decalcified. How about you scour it?" "But we didn't do anything!" Raff complained, crossing is arms over his chest. Georgy non-too-gently kicked him under the table to shut him up but it was already too late. The pastor glared them down. "Didn't do anything." He echoed. "Then what happened to the benches on the graveyard or my steering wheel?" Georgy looked straight up into the pastor's eyes. The guy had it coming. "And can you prove any of these accusations?" He asked calmly. "Don't push your luck, son." The pastor whispered. Now it was Raff's turn to give Georgy a hard kick.

"In any event...", Mister Flick turned around and walked back to his desk. "Come to me later and I will provide you with the supplies required. Regardless of whether there is proof or no, it won't hurt you to do some good."

It was hard work. "This stuff smells bad enough to wake the dead." Georgy muttered under his breath and looked up to the cross above. "Uh, sorry." He mumbled, looked away from the Jesus statue and poked Raff in the shoulder. "What?!" Raff hissed. His hands were red and it looked like he was beginning to develop a rash, scrubbing away like a maniac. "This stuff's just not coming off. Are we sure this isn't just the marbling of the stone." "Pretty sure." Georgy responded. "Look up there. Quite dapper with that new halo, isn't he?" Raff wiped his sleeve across his forehead and nodded. "Fetching, even. Though it kinda feels weird, like..." Raff suddenly looked uncomfortable. "Like he deserves more, you know?" Georgy grinned at that. "Couldn't agree more." He said. "Just look up to the church tower tomorrow morning. Then everyone will have gotten what was coming to them."

"You're nuts.", Raff dead-panned when they met at the school gates the next morning. "How did you even get the tires up there? I mean, that was you, right?"

Georgy grinned wolfishly. "And that's not all." When Raff gave him a questioning look, he continued. "I borrowed my mother's typewriter and left a little note on the car." "Are we talking about the car I think we're talking about?" "The very same. Last night I first took of the tires and got the up the church tower – real heavy if you've got to get them up so high. Then I wrote a note: You may have a new steering wheel, but

66

you will still have as much trouble directing your car as you do directing your community. The tires have joined the steering wheel in its hiding spot and if you want to find out where that is, I suggest you look to our savior on the cross for answers." Raff stared at him, wide-eyed. "Remind me to never get on your bad side." He mumbled.

Just that moment, Wally rounded the corner. When he spotted the two of them, he quickened his step considerably. "Were you at school last night, George?" He asked, still out of breath. "No, I wasn't." Georgy said. "Why do you ask?" "Because my old man almost caught someone sneaking through the hallways last night." "What, really?" Asked Raff. Wally told them that his dad had gotten news that there had been something wrong with the heater. The old thing went on the fritz sometimes and it hadn't been the first time he'd taken a nightly trip over to the school to fix it. Just when he had switched on the lights, two people, likely male were making their way around a corner. He chased them to the men's restroom and just so managed to catch one of them by the sleeve before they jumped out the window. "The guys managed to get away anyway, but dad tore off a piece of his jacket."

"Jeepers.", mumbled Raff. "Maybe it was a deal going on." Said Georgy. "Where's the piece of fabric now?" "At my place." Wally responded. "On its way to the closest trashcan, no doubt." "We should take a look at it during recess." "Sure thing, Sherlock."

"Here it is.", Wally said quietly, peering out into the hallway. Mister Woodman was at school and his mother was at the hairdresser's but both of them were known to drop in at the most inconvenient of times. "Fancy-shmancy.", Georgy said thoughtfully, stroking the fabric between his fingers. "Almost looks like the stuff my confirmation suit is made out of." "You're right!", Raff exclaimed. Wally frogged him in the arm and gestured to be more quiet, then he shrugged. "Yeah, the guy was wearing a suit." "What, how'd you know that?" Raff asked, rubbing his arm. "My dad saw them, remember? Even made a joke about how they probably were two fruits on a mid-night outing." "Why didn't you say so in the first place?" Raff gave Wally a good long glare. Wally shrugged again and grinned at Raff in mock-innocence. "You seemed so into playing detective, I didn't want to ruin that for ya." Raff snorted and took the fabric out of Georgy's hands. "Yeah, whatever. It's still interesting." "True." Georgy rejoined. " The question is: who'd wear a suit like that – to a late-night drug deal no less?" "Someone who needs to impress his buyers?" "Yeah, which is why he meets them in a middle school. C'mon, Raff." "Okay, okay." Raff muttered, staring at the strip of fabric like he could will it to give up its secrets. "Maybe... Maybe the guy was wearing a suit anyway. Like, my dad wears a suit to work – maybe it's someone who works in some official capacity." "Maybe a teacher?" Georgy whispered. "A teacher?" Wally echoed, raising his brows. "You think that's likely? Ballsy move, bringing that stuff where they work." "Yeah, but on the flipside..." Georgy mumbled. "Why do it at school at all? I mean, I've been wondering that for a while now – and teachers have keys, know the building and know it's very unlikely someone will walk in on them." "Not as unlikely as some would think." Raff chuckled as he put the piece of fabric back where they

68

had found it. On their way back to the classroom, they suspiciously glanced at every teacher wearing a suit.

Friday went by in a flash. A strange tingly feeling ad settled in the pit of Georgy's stomach and just wouldn't go away. Just thinking about how he was going to be at Anna's place the next day was simultaneously exciting and terrifying.

Georgy had never been invited somewhere, save for with his parents, once or twice. Birthday parties didn't count, either, this was different. This was a girl who wanted to see him and only him specifically. The thought alone was enough to make his palms sweaty. He didn't have that many fancy clothes, let alone anything that would have impressed a rich girl like Anna. Standing in front of his closet, staring at the meager selection within, he felt like was going to lose it. With something between a sigh and a grunt of frustration, he slammed the door shut. No use fussing over it now. Some nice jeans and a dress shirt would have to suffice.

Very briefly, he glanced at the suit his mother had bought for his confirmation, all snug under its plastic cover. It had been a little wide when he'd gotten it but his mother had said it'd fit just fine once he'd fill out a bit. In the end, she had had to refit it for him. Then again, maybe a suit was a little much. He didn't want Anna to think he was some try-hard.

Realizing that he was fussing again, he went to the living room to distract himself. As he'd already gone through all his books for the month, he grabbed a hold of the next best thing – the community newspaper – and plopped down on the couch. It appeared the pastor's tires had been recovered from the top of the church tower, but the article made no mention of the steering wheel. That could mean one of two things: Either the man hadn't figured it out yet or he was too embarrassed to admit that the thing had been hanging over his head the entire time and he hadn't noticed. Georgy grinned to himself.

Saturday morning went by painfully slow. Not one to get up before noon most weekend days, Georgy had been wide awake uncommonly early. He spent some time in the kitchen but didn't eat much, then he went to his room where he sat at his desk but couldn't think of anything he wanted to do. The only distraction, such as it was, was that his mother came in around eleven and ordered him to vacuum the living room. He suggested that his brother could help out as well, to no avail. His mother insisted that Tony was too young still and Georgy had the sneaking suspicion that he would always be.

After lunch, which went by much like breakfast in the sense that Georgy mostly poked at his food instead of eating it, Raff and Wally came for a visit. "You nervous?" Wally asked, when they were all sat on the carpet in Georgy's room. "No. Not at all." It was an obvious lie but Georgy didn't feel like talking about it. "Why would I be?" Wally shrugged and gave him a searching look. Raff, on the other hand, seemed entirely oblivious. "Broads like to play hard to get, so you gotta be persistent. I suggest you flirt with her until she kisses you!" "Even if it's only to shut you up." Wally interjected. "Whatever man, he needs a plan of attack." Raff said and it almost looked like he was pouting. "Plan of attack? Am I storming a castle?" "In a sense?" Raff mumbled, rubbing the back of his neck. "I mean you gotta decide if you wanna take the place over or, you know, just plunder the vault." "Good thing that nobody asked you." Georgy hissed. His face felt strangely hot. "Yeah, yeah." Raff grumbled. "I was just kidding anyway."

"What's really important is finding out if she knows where Kevin gets his stuff." Georgy mumbled. "And how will you go about that? I'm guessing being direct about it isn't much of an option." Wally asked. "Well, who knows?" Raff said, leaning back on his hands. "Heard smoking pot makes you stupid." "You been smoking pot, Raff?" "Ha ha." "Anyway, I'm hoping something will come up when we talk." Georgy mused. "Maybe the conversations will naturally develop that way." He scratched his head and couldn't really believe that he had just said that. "Regardless of what happens on that particular front, I hope it all turns out." Wally said, patting Georgy on the shoulder. "Yeah." Raff agreed. "Someone who can come up with a thorough plan like that to get back at the pastor will have no trouble getting some information from a girl. Just try making it extremely nice instead of extremely vindictive."

"By the way, I didn't read anything on the steering wheel in the community newspaper." Raff informed him a while later. "You think the guy still hasn't noticed?" Georgy nodded as though deep in thought. In reality, he had already spent a good long time trying to figure that one out. "I think..." He began slowly. "He knows where it is. I think he's trying to lure us into a trap." "A trap?" Wally's eyebrows had shot up so high that they were almost touching his hairline. "It's what I'd do, in his place." "What do you mean?" "Well..." He looked at Wally. "It doesn't really matter to you. You go to a different church. Raff, on the other hand..." "Yeah?" Raff ground out impatiently. "What? What?" "He might watch us on Sunday. Just don't look up at the cross. Act normal." "I might just be looking up in religious contemplation." Raff said, grinning. Georgy shook his head. "Better not risk it." "Maybe you should just not take that many risks with your pranks." Wally said dryly. Georgy pretended not to hear.

When Georgy left the house around six thirty in the evening, he was very tense. He had told his mother that he was likely going to spend the night at Wally's place because they were going to watch a movie and he didn't know how long it was going to be.

In reality, he was sitting on his bike, riding down the highway to the village. 'Just what's the matter with me, anyhow?' He thought his heart racing in his chest. 'There's no reason to be so nervous. She only invited me over because I helped her out. No reason to be nervous at all. Right?' And it didn't stop there. Very briefly, he managed to distract himself with the scenery, then he went right back to it. 'Sure, I want her to like me. If I could impress her, that would be awesome.' He sighed heavily. 'Not that it matters. No chance in hell that she'd ever... And would I even want that? Jeez, what's the matter with me? No way she'd ever be interested in some fourteen-year-old nobody loser kid. Okay, I'll be fifteen in a few months, but still! Don't girls like that usually go for cool older guys?' He shook his head to chase away the thought and almost fell off his bike. In the distance, he could already see the house on the hill.

The las bit of the way he pushed his bike and it felt like with every step he took, his feet were getting heavier. Anna's house loomed over the village, from where it sat on a hill on the outskirts. A steep, winding road lead up to an imposing iron gate. It was almost dark out and the only thing to be heard, were a few birds chirping. Georgy peeked through the iron bars. Behind them lay a mansion the likes of which he had thus far only seen in movies, tall, painted in brilliant white and immaculately maintained. Only a few of the many windows were lit up and he briefly pictured it illuminated in its entirety. The electrical bill alone would likely have sufficed to pay the rent for his entire flat. 'Dasher' it said on a big sign, right beneath a black doorbell. Georgy felt his palms beginning to sweat again and his heart beating in his throat, when he rung it.

For a few seconds, the only thing that happened was that Georgy could feel his heart hammering in his chest. "Yes?" Came a squeaky voice, crackling through the speakers. Georgy almost flinched at the sound. "Uh, hi?" He croaked and cleared his throat. "My name is George Thomson and I'm here to meet Anna." He almost said that he was there for a date but thought better of it. Briefly, it was almost suspiciously quiet on the other side, then the door swung open without so much as a sound. For the second time that day, Georgy noted how all of that stuff was only supposed to happen in movies, as he strolled down the cobbled path until he came to a fork in it. One side lead up to an enormous garage, the other to the entrance, which was just as big as everything else in that place appeared to be. When Georgy approached it, he realized he had no idea what to do next.

In the doorframe stood a tall man in a suit, who quickly gave him a once over.

"Follow me.", He said, gesturing in a round-about way at the path, the door and himself. The entrance hall was almost empty, except for a strange sculpture-type thing in its center. To Georgy it looked like little more than bent piece of scrap-metal but then again, he didn't know anything about art. When he looked up, he saw that there were a ton of tiny lamps integrated into the ceiling. It looked a little like stars. "There will be time to appreciate the architecture later, Sir." Nobody had ever called Georgy 'Sir' before and the sound of the word alone was enough to startle him into motion. He had heard that the house on the hill was like a gateway to another world and with how out of place he suddenly felt, he was inclined to agree.

The man lead him into a room with a curved staircase. Before Georgy had the time to turn around, someone called out to him from the second floor. "Yo George. Get yourself up here." Georgy looked up. Anna was grinning at him, standing on one of those indoor-balconies, which he had only ever seen at the mall. She was wearing a dark sweater and her hair was pinned up. When Georgy climbed up the stairs, Anna turned to the strange man in his suit. "Thanks, Arty." She said. "That'll be all for now. I'll call for you when we get hungry." Georgy looked back at the man in surprise, but he was already gone.

"Was that a servant?" Georgy asked. "He prefers being called 'Butler'." Anna said and smiled at him. "C'mon already, or are you waiting for the manservants to roll out the sedan chair?" "Sedan chairs don't roll." Georgy mumbled a little embarrassed and followed Anna down a hallway.

A few moments later, he was standing in her room. He gave it his best effort, but he just couldn't not be awed by the sight. "Wow." He muttered under his breath. "You like it?" Anna asked not expecting a response. "Have a seat." "It's amazing." Georgy said, carefully lowering himself onto a fancy couch. Anna's room was more of a flat than a room. There were multiple doors leading to other rooms, two of them ajar. There likely was a bathroom behind one of them, judging by the smell of perfume and other stuff that reminded him of his mom that came from there. Something from behind door number two emitted a soft glow, so maybe it was the bedroom. Two more doors were closed. Georgy was deeply impressed. "Are you thirsty?" "Uh, sure." "Anything in particular?" When Georgy didn't say anything and just stared at Anna with his mouth hanging open like a fish out of water, she seemed to take pity on him. "How does a Coke sound?" "That would be nice." "One coke, coming right up." Anna opened one of the doors and flipped the light switch. He could hear her rummaging through the cupboards inside. So it was a kitchen. He stifled a sigh and reviewed what he had accomplished thus far. Though he had actually kind of liked it when Anna had made a decision for him, he also hadn't forgotten about his plan to let the conversation to progress naturally. He silently cursed his own awkwardness and shook his head. Step one: Start talking.

Anna came back, handed him a glass and lifted hers. "Cheers." She said. "Yeah, cheers." They slipped a bit of coke. Georgy felt ridiculous. "So tell me, how did you do the key thing?" Anna asked, nudging his shoulder with her elbow. Georgy could feel his ears heating up and hoped to god that Anna wouldn't notice. "Well." He started. "It was actually pretty easy." "What's with the humble act?" Anna laughed and tipped her head to the side. After a moment of silence, Georgy realized that was likely supposed to mean 'Go ahead'. "I know a guy. He gave me the key to the supply room. I drilled through the lock and put the Teddy on the shelf." He shrugged. "And that's already it." "Yeah, real easy." Anna was still smiling at him and he just couldn't help himself but look at her. The best part was that it wasn't creepy this time. "How did you get into the building?" She asked. "Through a window on the ground floor. I do it all the time." He immediately realized that he had said too much. Anna's head shot around and a wide grin spread across her face. "So you so that a lot, do you? Break into the school to mess with things?" "Uh..." Georgy stuttered. "Once or twice?" "Is it at all possible..." Anna began and he could hear the laughter ringing in her voice. "That you had, oh, I don't know, something to do with that incident in the teacher's lounge?" Because she looked at him in that way, like she were genuinely interested and maybe even a little impressed, Georgy just couldn't stop himself. "Yeah." He said. "That was me." Anna laughed voicelessly, shaking her head as if she couldn't believe it. "Wow." She mumbled. "You know... You were the talk of the school. Seriously, all the girls in my homeroom were dying to meet you. They thought you were the coolest." She considered for a moment and suddenly her expression changed. "You're not having me on, are you? Taking credit for some other person's credit would be seriously so lame." "No, of course not!" Georg blurted. He would lie if he said that he wasn't offended. To prove that he was telling the truth he began explaining exactly how he had done it. The only part he left out was where he had gotten the key to the teacher's lounge. "So you see..." He finished with a sweeping gesture. "Boyle's law. I didn't make it up." "I believe you. You didn't make up physics. Unless you're taking advantage of the fact that I'm terrible at it and that law doesn't exist to begin with." "I could prove it to you." Georgy said stubbornly. Anna just laughed again. "Relax. I said I believe you, didn't I? Besides, I can't pay attention when I'm hungry. How about we go find Arty?" Georgy nodded. "Sounds good." "You go to the dining room, I'll pick out something tasty. Do you like lamb?" "Um, sure." Georgy has never ever had lamb before. On his way through the lounge, he yet again realized how different her world was from his. There was nothing her parents couldn't afford. There were months when his mother didn't know how to make rent.

The dining room table was set, and a lady dressed as a maid carried out their food on a tray after Arty had made sure that everything was to Anna's taste.

After a while, when they were alone again, Georgy couldn't stand the curiosity any longer. "How many servants do you have anyway?" He asked. "Cook, maid, driver and Arty. Makes four." "What, no gardener?" Georgy went on, suspiciously prodding at his salad with a fork. He'd never had a multi-course meal before. "Eh, you know what they say about gardeners." Anna made a dismissive gesture." That would be super creepy, especially now that my parents aren't home." "Where are they, then?" If Georgy were to ever bring a girl home, his mother probably wouldn't leave them alone for even a moment, gushing and fussing. He shuddered inwardly. "Oh you know, mom's somewhere in NYC and dad's off building some resort in... Australia, I think it was." "Oh, okay." Georgy had that strange feeling again, like what was going on wasn't real, that he didn't belong on that long table in the dining room with its fancy plates and heaps of differently sized cutlery. Anna chuckled. "That probably sounds weird to you, but my parents aren't home so frequently that I can't even keep track of where they go." "That's fine." He mumbled. "Things just work different up here." "What do you mean?" "You know, with the money and all that." "You think?" Anna seemed to think about that for a moment, the she said: "You know, that stuff isn't all rainbows and sunshine, either." 'Yeah, but mostly.' Georgy thought grudgingly. Anna didn't notice the shift in the mood and went on. "It's a real bummer, sometimes. They say money can't buy you friendship but it sure does attract a lot of jerks. I can't remember dating anyone who didn't just turn out to be a money-grubbing piece of trash." "What, really?" Georgy found that hard to believe. "But you're so..." He trailed off. "Yeah?" Anna raised her brows at him but her smile wasn't fading. "Do tell." Georgy thought hard. If there had ever been an inconvenient time for his mind to go

78

blank, this was without a doubt it. "You're funny, for a start." He said, scratching his head. "And you like superheroes. And you're nice and not at all stuck up as far as I can tell, and you got a wicked kick, so..." He faltered. Anna was just staring at him now, she wasn't even smiling anymore. There was a moment of silence. "Huh." Said Anna. "That's not wat I expected at all. I thought you were just going to tell me I was pretty." "That too..." Georgy stuttered. They were quiet again, eating their salad. "So, you like girls who are into superheroes?" Anna asked, grinning mischievously when Arty brought out the tomato soup. "I guess." Georgy shrugged. "I just haven't met many girls who were." Anna's grin widened. "Oh, I definitely am. Even got Batman bedsheets." She paused for dramatic effect, then she said. "Maybe I could show them to you later." For a moment, Georgy considered diving face first into his bowl. At least Anna wouldn't be able to see the furious blush on his face that way.

"So, are there any other secrets you have?" "Uh, what do you mean?" "Well, I mean what else did you pull?" Georgy didn't know what to say to that. He already felt like he had said too much. "Oh, c'mon, George. Please? I'm not gonna tell anyone. Promise." "Well, I'd hope so. I'll get suspended otherwise. Already told you way too much." Anna put her hand on his shoulder, tilted her head and exaggeratedly batted her eyelashes. "Pretty please?" Georgy felt like he couldn't move. "Well, uh..." He cleared his throat and started talking. The food was delicious and they chatted away, laughing and giggling like old friends until suddenly the door was flung open.

79

A young man came in. Georgy immediately felt like there was something wrong with him. Then he smelt the alcohol. Thez guy was maybe twenty-five. He looked dirty, kind of disheveled and pale as he stood there, swaying in place until his eyes found Anna. "You got more of the stuff?" He slurred. He seemed to have trouble focusing. Georgy felt like he was frozen in place. Just a couple moments ago he had been having a great time, but the atmosphere had shifted so dramatically that he suddenly wasn't sure if maybe it wasn't all just a dream. "Who's that guy?" The man asked, vaguely gesturing in Georgy's direction and almost knocking himself off balance. Anna's expression had turned strangely stiff. "A friend." She said and glared at him, then she added, matter-of-factly: "You're drunk." The statement awkwardly hung in the air, as they all seemed to marvel at its implications. "Sorry George. My brother." Anna said. "Hey." The man grumbled. "No one ever tell you it's rude to talk 'bout people like they'rnt there? So you got more stuff or what?" "No Lars, I told you I wasn't going to do that anymore. Now leave already." Lars narrowed his eyes at her. "I live here too, you know." "You freeload is more like it." "Now listen here, you little floosy." Lars took two wobbly steps forward. "If I tell mom that you invited your..." He pointed at George. "Him over without her permission, you'll be in deep." "Yeah? And if I tell her you spend your days smoking and drinking yourself to death instead of looking for a job you'll be in deeper." Though Anna had clenched her fists by her sides, her voice lacked conviction. Georgy noticed that her hands were shaking and judging by the sly smile that had crept onto Lars' face he had as well. "You sure about that?" Lars almost whispered, taking another step toward her. "You think she will believe you? You think she

80

will believe you over me?" That moment Georgy remembered something. Something Anna had said during their first meeting: 'My mom will kill me if the school sends another bill.' Sure, he had thought it was strange even then, seeing how her family was pretty much swimming in money but now things began falling into place. "Tomorrow you'll go to Kevin and get me some." Lars stated as though he were summarizing a business meeting. "No, I won't!" Anna had tears in her eyes and her voice was shaking with anger and frustration. "Go buy that shit yourself!" "How about you shut it before I lose my temper!?" Lars shot back. "Leave her alone." Georgy was aware, in a way that the words had come out of his mouth just as he knew that he must have gotten up at some point, although he couldn't remember deciding to do either. Lars turned his back on Anna, his blood-shot eyes cantering on him instead. He was only a bit shorter than Lars, though likely 40 pounds lighter. "What?" Lars asked. "You gonna play hero? I could blow your head off, you fricking twink." Georgy's mouth felt strangely dry and a high-pitched buzzing noise was rising in his ears. "Leave her alone or I'll..." "You'll what?" Lars was quickly closing the distance between them, a predatory glint in his eyes but before he could throw a singly punch, Georgy had wound up and buried his fist in the pit of Lars' stomach. In a way that could have been comical, if everybody present hadn't been under varying degrees of shock and surprise, he slumped forward, making a noise reminiscent of a beach ball deflating and crumpled to the floor.

Georgy was the first to snap out of his stupor. "Oh god, I'm sorry." He stammered. "I didn't mean to do that." He was just about to bend over to try and haul

81

the guy back to his feet, when Anna practically threw herself at him. Sobbing, she buried her face in his chest and Georgy could feel hot tears soaking through the fabric of his shirt. With a bang, the door was thrown open and Arty and another man were suddenly standing in front of them. Arty's eyes wandered from Anna crying to Lars' prone form on the floor next to them to Georgy who was standing in the middle of the room, petrified like a deer caught in the headlights. "What..." Arty began, his voice clipped and controlled. "Is going on here." Georgy was drawing a complete blank. He numbly looked down at his fist, still half-ways up in the air. "Lars was having one of his moments again." Anna said with unconcealed disgust in her voice. "If George hadn't..." She angrily shook her head and leaned back toward Georgy. To everybody's surprise, she closed the remaining distance between them and planted a big kiss on his cheek. "Thank you." She said. "He had it coming."

Arty and the other man who turned out to be the driver helped Lars who was still breathing hard back to his feet. Georgy was distractedly surveying his fist in something akin to awe. The thing literally packed a punch. "We shall escort Mister Lars back to his room. He likely won't accost you again today, Misses Anna." "Thank you, Arty." Anna said now that she mostly had her voice back under control again. Arty inclined his head, then he looked at Georgy. "It may strike you as rude, considering... services rendered but it would be prudent should you return home sooner rather than later, I think." "Yes, he'll leave soon but not yet." Anna said, pulling on Georgy's sleeve for emphasis. "Right?" "Uh, sure. Of course." He muttered. Definitely a dream. Had to be.

A little later, they were sitting on the sofa in Anna's room again. "My brother's a dink." Anna opened unceremoniously. "He got caught buying a couple of times, so dad said he'd write him out of his will if he didn't sober up." Georgy marveled at the fact that there were families were that actually worked as a threat. "So he asked me to get him more. Demanded, more like." "And you didn't tell your dad?" Georgy asked. "He's never home, and my mom..." Tears were beginning to rise in her eyes yet again and Georgy reached for her hand. "That's why you were buying from Kevin." "How do you know that?" "Your brother said." Georgy said maybe a little too quickly. Anna sniffed. "Just sounded weird the way you said it." Georgy shrugged and avoided her eyes. He didn't want Anna to find out the real reason for why he was there, especially when she had already been having a bad day. To his surprise, she gave him an apologetic smile. "Sorry, if that sounded paranoid." She mumbled. "I'm just worried, you know? That stuff is illegal and if people knew I..."

"I'm not gonna tell anyone, promise." Georgy said and when it suddenly was Anna, who avoided looking at him, he added. "Look, now both of us have a secret that could potentially ruin..." He interrupted himself. "I mean, it's not like you take the stuff yourself. Right?" Even with her face red and smudged with make-up, Anna was beautiful. Georgy chased away the thought. How could he think about how pretty she was when she was so clearly upset? Anna shook her head. "Of course not. You know what happens when you get busted for possessions?" 'Good.', Georgy thought. 'That makes things easier. Seems I was wrong on all accounts there.' He squeezed her hand sympathetically. "Makes you wonder how Kevin managed to not get busted yet. I'm pretty sure his parents were siblings." Anna mustered a half-hearted snort at that. "I know, right? The guy who sells him that stuff has to be really desperate." Georgy's breath caught and he forced a cough to cover it up. This was his chance. "So, uh, some dumb high schooler trying to make a quick buck?" Anna shook her head. "No – at least I don't think so. He said something about a Frenchman he was going to meet, one time when Lars wanted something different, you know?" "Huh." Georgy tried to sound only mildly interested but in his head, the gears were turning.

They sat together for a while longer, Georgy holding Anna's hand in his, her head against his shoulder. He could just imagine what Raff would say if he could see him right now. It was weird how that guy managed to be a pain without actually being present sometimes. It was around eleven, when he finally found his voice again. "Hey, uh, I really should get home now. Is... Is that okay with you?" Anna lifted her head of his shoulder and rubbed at her neck. When she spoke, she sounded pretty normal again. "Sure it is. Hope the evening was at least kind of salvageable to you." Georgy gave her his best smile. "Are you kidding? Just wait until I tell the valley folk that there are actual people living up here and it isn't just a facade, like in these old western flicks." "You sure about that?" Anna asked the familiar glint back in her eyes. "For all you know all this junk could turn back into pumpkins, lizards and mice come midnight." Georgy cocked a brow at her. "Kind of a step down from comic books, don't you think." "Fairytales? Definitely." She gave him a smile that almost made his insides melt. "They'll never come true. But sometimes people do heroic things. See you on Monday."

He pushed his bike on the way home. A million thoughts were cluttering up his mind. It had been amazing when she had told him that she thought he was cool, just up until that point when her dink of a brother had shown up. On the other hand, he wouldn't have been able to play hero if he hadn't. He had basically knocked out an adult – just thinking about that made his stomach do somersaults, especially considering that he usually avoided confrontation. He was neither that strong nor was he usually brave enough to risk a busted lip anyway. Now, however, he felt different.

The next morning began with the obligatory trip to church. Georgy and Raff sat next to each other on one of the benches further in the back. Georgy immediately noticed that the Jesus statue seemed to be missing its halo. He and Raff grinned at each other. "Remember not to look up once Mr. Flick comes in." Georg whispered. "Yeah, yeah." Raff rolled his eyes. "So how did it go last night?"

Raff's eyes looked like they were about to pop out of their sockets at any moment, once they had found a spot on one of the benches on the graveyard after the service and Georgy had finished his story. "So you punched him out. *You* punched him out? And then she kissed you? Are you sure you didn't fall off your bike on your way to her place and hit your head?" Raff gave a bark of incredulous laughter but when Georgy gave him a poisonous glare, he sobered up a bit. "Okay, okay." He wheezed. "Geez, little Georgy all grown up. Just wait till Wally hears of this." "Ha ha." Georgy grumbled. "Very funny. And besides, it wasn't that great at all. It was just a kiss on the cheek. And I didn't tell her the truth. I didn't tell her that we've been watching her." "What, you think we'll rat?" Georgy shrugged uncomfortably. Raff just laughed. "Yes, you've discovered our evil plan. Wally and I have conspired to keep you sad and single forever." Georgy mumbled something unintelligible, though abruptly cut himself off when Raff kicked him in the shin. In truth, that wasn't really what he'd been worried about at all.

Scratching his head, he sighed. "You know what I'd like to know?" He asked. "How you spent the entire evening sitting on her bed, yet still didn't even get a kiss?" Now it was Georgy's time to give Raff a good kick. "No. I just can't figure out who the Frenchman is."

Chapter 5 Jingle-Bell Rock

"The Frenchman.", Wally mused, after Georgy had given him the sit-rep during recess on Monday. "Lamest villain name ever." Raff supplied helpfully. Wally gave Georgy a questioning look. "Well, if it is a teacher…" Georgy nodded. "Either he teaches French or he is French." "The principal is French." Raff pointed out. "But he's also got enough money to turn his office into a golf course." Wally replied, shaking his head. "Maybe the principal has an evil-" but Raff never got to finish that sentence.

"My, my, lookey there. Told you we'd miss all the scheming if we went to lunch." Georgy and Raff turned to see. Georgy swallowed hard. It was Anna, arms locked with a blond girl in a wide skirt, coming toward them. A shamelessly wide grin spread across Raff's face, Wally raised his brows and Georgy bashfully inspected his shoes. "Hello there." Anna said, nodding encouragingly at Georgy. If Wally hadn't subtly pinched his shoulder, he may have missed it altogether. "H-hi there, Anna.", he muttered awkwardly. It felt like Saturday had been impossibly long ago, a dream, almost, and Georgy barely managed to look Anna in the eyes. Anna clapped her hands and looked around. "So. Who are your friends?" It took Georgy a moment to realize that she was unmistakably talking to him. "That's Wally and Raff. Same homeroom." "Cool. Oh, this is my friend. She's your age." Raff was the first to recover his voice, though for some reason it seemed to suddenly be two octaves deeper. "That's fine." He drawled, with all the smarmy appeal a 14-year-old could possibly muster. "You may stand near us anyway. Least we can do is make sure you have a good time if you're already missing lunch for our sakes." If Georgy hadn't been embarrassed before he certainly was now, and Wally seemed to feel the same, judging by how hard he cuffed Raff between the shoulder blades. It was almost funny, the way Raff spun around in a flash, rubbing at his back, his voice bouncing back to its usual pitch. "What was that for?" He hissed, angrily. "Wasp." Wally said with a shrug and a coy smile. "Awful early in the year for wasp, don't you think?" Raff groused. "Must be all the acid rain." Wally said wryly.

"Regular comedians, your friends." Anna said and looked from one to the other. "But you know, Raff..." "It's Ralf, actually, but you can call me whatever ugh-" Raff cut himself off when Wally flicked his ear. "Whatever my friends call me." He finished haltingly. "Which is Raff." Wally and Georgy rolled their eyes in unison. Georgy briefly wondered if girls were actually into that act. "So Raff, like I said..." Anna bristled and Raff deflated like a punctured floating aid. That probably meant no. "Our usual haunt had a burst pipe so there isn't much competition." Then she turned to Georgy. "Thanks for last night." She said. "Also, thanks for showing my brother what for." Anna glanced over at his friends. She probably could tell that he had already told them by the way they didn't react at all. "Lisa knows, too." She said quickly, just when Georgy realized why she had said what she had said in the first place and what it exactly it was that she had told Lisa. It was like they had reached a non-verbal understanding; 'You keep your friends in check and I will do the same with mine.' Anna would make a fine politician one day, Georgy thought wryly. "So how's he?" He asked in a tone that didn't match his thoughts. "Oh, he's fine, I guess. He just was, you know, black-out drunk. Doesn't even remember you knocking him on his butt." Georgy felt very relieved to hear that. He'd already spent half a night worrying over what to do if Lars came for him. Lisa interrupted his thoughts, when she turned to Wally. "You're the janitor's son, right?" She asked. Georgy and Raff looked at each other. Even though he would never admit it, Wally was a little embarrassed over his father's job. Not embarrassed, per se, just a bit annoyed by constantly being associated with the guy who unclogged the toilets. Since Mister Woodman had also managed to somehow get stuck with the role of Middle school-vigilante, Wally also regularly got in trouble with the kids his dad busted for breaking rules and general mischief. "If there's anything broken in your classroom or something you should take that to him personally." Wally said dryly. Lisa looked taken aback for a moment, then she shook her head. "No, no. He's just always so nice to us, is all." she said, her eyes warm. Wally's expression switched to an easy smile of the variety, that Georgy had secretly practiced in the mirror yet always failed to replicate. "Yeah? That's a switch." A slight blush crept onto Lisa's cheeks. "People ask you to bring him messages a lot?" Anna asked, sounding mildly interested. "Just the usual stuff." Wally said with a shrug. "My desk is wobbly, the window won't close, screw your dad, nobody said you couldn't feed firecrackers to the class mascots, that sort of thing." "Oh no." Lisa said, wide-eyed. "Why would anyone do something like that?" Briefly taken aback, Wally gave her a warm smile. "I was just kidding." He said.

They were all quiet for a moment. "Would you like to go to the movies with us tonight?" Anna asked out of the blue. "Sounds good." Wally said almost immediately. "What are we watching?" "There is this new Disney movie: The Rescuers." "Cool." Wally said, still grinning. "Animated movies are awesome." Georgy almost laughed out loud. What a joke. "How about you?" Anna asked. Raff, quite unlike his usual self, looked off to the side. "Can't." He said glumly. "Today's my old man's birthday." "Oh, don't worry about it." said sympathetically. "You win some, you lose some." "Yeah." Wally said, imitating's tone but grinning. "You win some you lose some." Raff tried to make a rude hand gesture without the girls noticing. "You?" Anna asked, turning to Georgy, who had been staring at his shoes for a while now. "Don't have any time either. Sorry."

Raff's face lit up a little at those words. "You got somewhere to be?" Wally asked. Maybe Georgy was imagining it, but he was pretty sure that Wally didn't believe him. In any event, he would rather have bitten off his tongue right there and then than admitting the truth in front of everybody. It was simple really, he couldn't afford it. The ticket would already be expensive enough by itself. Add bus fare and snacks... Not to mention, he didn't know if Anna expected him to pay for her- but he couldn't ask either because what if she hadn't even meant it in that way? Like a date? He mumbled something vague about having to babysit his brother while his parents were out on the town and prayed to god that Wally and Raff wouldn't see right through his lie. Usually the Thomson family went out for dinner exactly once per week, on Friday evenings to a small, cheap German place down the street that was pretty good and sold ridiculous huge schnitzels and fries. "Well, that sucks." Anna said and she actually sounded disappointed. "Too bad." Raff said. He obviously didn't mean it, the way he was barely fighting off a grin. "Another time, then." Anna looked directly at George, and he felt a little like he was being x-rayed. Briefly, he wondered what it was she was looking for and quickly looked away. "Sure, another time sounds great." He mumbled.

That moment, the school bell rang. Anna cast a disgruntled look in the direction of the other students. "Ugh, I absolutely hate all the bustle." They began moving in the direction of the building. "And every time you're having a good time, that stupid bell rings. Makes me want to blow my ears off." "How about blowing up the bell instead?" Georgy supplied hopefully. He quite liked Anna's ears. They went really well with her face. Anna slowed down a bit and quirked an eyebrow at him. "Blow up the bell?" She repeated and it sounded like a challenge. "Don't be ridiculous, there's no way." Georgy pursed his lips, looked at Wally, looked at Raff and nodded. "You're crazy." Raff said but it lacked all venom – instead it just sounded mildly amused. "Not again." Wally mumbled half-heartedly. "Doubt you'll need me to give you the Spiel again but if my dad catches us, I'm a dead man." "Where will you even get explosives?" Anna asked incredulously. "What are we talking about?" Lisa wondered. When nobody answered her question, Anna half-sighed, half-sniggered, threaded her fingers through her friend's and gave her hand a tug. "I'll tell you later." She said mirthfully, and in a louder voice added: "We gotta go anyway, later Georgy. Wally. Ralf." "Raff." Raff said quietly, pouting. Anna just grinned, twinkle in her eye and with a flip of her hair she turned her back on

91

them and disappeared into the crowd, in tow. They watched them go for a few more moments, Raff mumbling something about how that could have gone better. Wally rolled his eyes. "Your own   fault." He said. "Has that jerk-act ever actually worked for you or what?" When Raff didn't respond and just testily kicked at some pebbles on the ground, Wally rolled his eyes again and turned to George. "And what was that bull about babysitting? Your parents never go out by themselves." Georgy stifled a sigh. Busted. "I don't have the money." He admitted. Wally nodded and Raff looked surprised. "Man, why didn't you just say something?" He asked. "I'd spot you no problem." Georgy gave a slow exhale. No, he decided grimly, that would be even worse. He didn't have to answer, however, because Wally, who had clasped a hand over Raff's shoulder just shook his head and asked. "You really wanna blow up the bell?" Raff looked confused and Georgy felt a little bad for him but as it was, he just gave Wally a grateful smile.

"You know how I, uh, liberated some supplies from the Chemlab? As a means of... deepening my understanding of the subject matter at home, of course." He couldn't help but chuckle at the ridiculous way Raff winked repeatedly at the words. "It's simple, really -." The other two rolled their eyes but Georgy went on, undeterred. "We still have some charcoal at home and, you know..." "I don't actually." Wally said, looking slightly annoyed. "Me neither." Raff said. "Unless we're going to have a grill party with the school bell, that is." He turned to Georgy and gave him a funny look. "That isn't what you meant though, is it?" "No, it isn't." Georgy muttered. "And it doesn't matter anyway, cause I have no   idea   how   I   could   ignite   that   stuff remotely." "Ignite?" Raff echoed, looking strangely pale for a moment. "You know." He said when he had regained his composure. "You have that strange talent of making me feel like an idiot." And exchanging a nervous glance with Wally, he added. "And making me fret for my safety." "I fret for your safety when I see you with a pair of scissors." Wally joked but he looked uneasy. "Oh, can it, you two." Georgy rejoined. As entertaining as their squabbling was, sometimes it just got on his nerves. "I'm only making a bit of gunpowder – A tiny bit for my purposes. Nothing to worry about." "And you gotta figure out how to ignite it remotely." Raff said. Georgy thoughtfully scratched his head. "It would be easiest with one of those firecrackers, you know, the small red ones. I still got some from New Year's." "But you gotta ignite it remotely." Raff repeated, looking confused yet again. "Although I don't really get why you don't just use a match." Georgy snorted indignantly. "'Course just lighting the thing would be easier but it would lack the flair, don't you think?" He shook his head. "I mean, I could just disassemble the entire thing, too. But that would be boring. Nobody would notice, class wouldn't even be delayed." They had reached the staircase leading up to the second floor and fell silent as they climbed it.

Wally and Georgy met again during homeroom but there was no trace of Raff. The two of them had pushed their desks together and were chatting quietly. Their homeroom teacher, Mister Moe, was having a late lunch in the front and didn't pay them any mind. "Figure out how to do it yet?" Wally asked without any preamble. "Yeah, I did." He said and looked up at the front desk. Mister Moe seemed entirely engrossed by his sandwich. "Where is Raff, though?" Wally raised his brows. "What, need an audience?" "No. Just don't wanna tell the story twice." Wally shrugged non-commitaly. "Trying to get Urs to go out with him. I don't think he'll be long. Urs has a short temper." "And Raff has no filter." Georgy chuckled.

They talked about the hardships of dating for a while and so it took until school was over for Georgy to get around to telling Wally what he was planning. When they were outside in the schoolyard, still no sign of Raff, he gave Wally the short version. "The idea with the match wasn't bad. I'll put the gunpowder in a matchbox – just a bit, don't want to blow up the school. Put in a firecracker, fuse-side sticking out. Gotta make that longer somehow, right? I'll just take the fuse off of another thing, attach that to a match and attach the match to the ringing mechanism. That way, the match will be lit when the bell rings. It burns down, lights the fuses and then -" He made a big gesture with his hands. "Kablooey!"

"I like the sound of that." The both of them whirled around. "Jiminy cricket." Georgy whispered in relief. "What's with the guilty faces?" Anna asked, doing her best to sound disapproving. "Makes me think you are hiding something." "I resent that." Wally said, with a wide grin. Anna turned to Georgy and though she was giving him the most charming of smiles, he suddenly felt nervous. "Got a surprise for you." She said and his stomach did a flip. "I asked our maid if she could babysit for you tonight. She said she wouldn't mind." Georgy felt the color drain from his face and he was pretty sure that Wally had gone stiff next to him. "That- er, that's awesome." He stuttered. Anna's face fell a little. "Uh, sorry." She said. "Aren't you- I mean, I guess I should have asked. I just-" "That's not it." The moment Wally cut her off, Georgy knew what was going to happen next. If Georgy had to guess, his face was probably a vibrant shade of crimson now and he pleadingly looked at Wally but it was too late. "See, Georgy's already used up all his allowance this month. That's why he can't go." Georgy stared at the floor. He wasn't sure what he was expecting would happen next but he didn't think it was going to be good, so he started by steeling himself. "Cool." Anna said. For a moment he was sure he must have misheard her and looked up despite himself. Anna smiled at him. "So it's a date, then." Now Georgy was sure that there was something wrong with his ears. "You know what?" She went on. "If I recall correctly, I owe you anyway. Is a ticket to the show and a large bag of popcorn sufficient compensation for punching out my brother?" Forget my ears, Georgy thought in amazement, I must be dreaming. "Ticket, small popcorn and some pop, I think." Wally said, with a nod. Georgy was pretty sure that he could have fried an egg on his own face by this point. Wally elbowed him in the side. "C'mon, are you waiting for her to write you an official invitation or something?" "I'd do it, too." Anna sniggered. "Even got some lovely scented paper." Georgy made a mental note to make sure those two wouldn't spend too much time together. He would probably never have a quiet moment again otherwise. "Okay." He said. "Great." Anna laughed and clapped her hands. "How about you, Wally?" "Sure." Wally replied. "Awesome. Pick you guys up around three? Just gotta tell we're on." "You drive?" Wally asked. "From time to time." Anna nodded. "Probably gonna recruit the driver for this, though. Want to tell me where you live so we can come get you?" She asked Georgy. "Graveldrive 51. Wally knows where that is."

"So how about you tell me what is supposed to go Kablooey now?" Georgy and Wally grinned at each other. "No can do, sorry." Georgy said. "Aw, come on, why not?" Anna got the cutest wrinkle between her brows when she pouted, Gorgy noticed. "We don't rightly know ourselves yet." Wally said simply. Anna nodded, satisfied with that answer. "Anyway. I gotta go." She had already taken a few steps away from them, when she turned around again. "See you guys tonight." She called back. "Looking forward to it!" "We do, too." They mumbled in unison but she probably didn't hear that anymore.

"Honestly, Wally." Georgy grumbled once he was sure she was out of earshot. "Did you have to embarrass me like that." Wally waved his hand dismissively. "Oh, get over yourself." He said. "I don't think she cared at all." "Yeah maybe, but it was still embarrassing." "Listen." Wally said and his tone became serious. "I honestly think you are the only one who's bothered by that money stuff. Anna seems cool. How about you just give her a chance?" Wally studied him for a moment, then he exhaled with a whistle. "And I don't think you should blow up the bell." "What?" Georgy stared at his friend like he'd grown a second head. Not blow up the bell? "But I already told Anna – well, sort of, anyways. And what happened to not wanting me to end up an old spinster?" "That's exactly my point, Anna obviously likes you, so why do it? I thought you didn't want to break things. You got something to prove?" Wally gave him a good long look, then he added: "Lately your pranks've been getting more and more... I don't know. Vicious, I guess. What are you doing?" Georgy didn't know how to response to that. Was it true? He stayed quiet.

The movies had been great. Once Georgy had collapsed onto his bed, he fondly thought of what had happened that afternoon, a blissful smile on his face.

At 03.30 sharp, the car had arrived. A big, black Mercedes. Georgy had purposefully walked up the road bit, so his parents or brother wouldn't be able to see him through the window. Georgy had never sat in a car like that. Just sitting in it had been enough to chase away the strange feeling he had had since talking to Wally that afternoon. Once in the theatre, he hadn't really been able to focus on the movie and had instead found himself glancing at Anna more often than not. He was pretty sure that it had been much the same with Wally, though Wally had at least been able to summarize the plot of the movie afterwards. (Something about talking mice and an orphan girl.) It had been fun, in any case, the time flying by so fast that he had almost been disappointed when the curtain fell. Then again, Anna had suggested they meet again the following day during recess, which was somewhat of a comfort.

Before falling asleep, his thoughts drifted back to the Frenchman. Who was he? A French teacher? He himself wasn't great at languages and only had scientific and technology-based electives. Maybe

Anna or would know something. He decided to ask them the next day.

"When are you going to do it?" Of course, they had told Raff of the plan with the matchbox. "Maybe tomorrow, or the day after – I'll figure it out. Gotta take the thing apart first. Gotta do it, so I'll know how to attach the matchbox. Took a piece of spring steel from an old Relais." "What is it and what does it do?" Raff asked his face completely neutral. "How about you start paying attention in class? Even if its distracting sitting behind Urs. How's that going, by the way?" Raff gave him a thumbs-down. "Quit trying to change the subject." He grumbled. "Or at least change it to something else. What is spring steel?" "It's like the switch of the relay. Made from spring steel. I'll braze that onto the hammer of the bell." "Cool." Raff said. "Even better because you're actually good at that stuff. Everything I make in shop class just ends up falling apart." "Only when you try picking it up. Which seems to be a common theme with you." Wally said with a lop-sided grin. "Gimme a break." Raff huffed indignantly but Georgy noticed the red splotches that were appearing on his neck. "You think you can do better with that chick?" "Who says I haven't already." "You didn't!" Raff exclaimed. Wally shrugged but there was a twinkle in his eyes. "Who knows? I don't kiss and tell." Raff didn't say anything for a moment, looking very satisfyingly gob smacked, then a grin spread across his face. "Geez." He mumbled. "Mom was right. It is the quiet ones you gotta watch out for." He turned to Georgy as if he was seeing him for the first time, eyes wide with wonder. "Does that mean you got Anna to make out with you, too?" Georgy didn't like being looked at that way at all and shifted uncomfortably in place. "Uh, why?" He wished he could take the words back as soon as they had left his mouth. "Pish, 'Why', he asks." Raff shook his head, oddly looking even more baffled than before. "I know you don't have much hands-on experience with it but isn't there any kissing in those books of yours?" "I don't read romance novels!" Georgy groused but he could feel his cheeks   heating   up.

That afternoon, he went to meet Wally. He rode his bike to the Woodmans' so Wally could give him the key and he'd be able to get into school to look at the bell.
"No." "What do you mean 'No'?" They were sitting in Wally's room, Wally resting his feet on the guitar he'd been practicing with before Georgy had come in and looking absolutely immovable. "No." He said again. "No dice, not gonna give you the key this time." Georgy almost didn't believe his ears. What had gotten into Wally lately – It was just going to be a harmless prank. "Like, forget Anna. Didn't you say that drug-guy had a knife? What if you run into him again, except without Philip to draw his attention or my dad around to chase him off?" Georgy thought on that for a moment. Sure, the stakes were up but he knew what he was doing – he changed his tactic. "You know I'll get into school with our without your help?" He said slyly, watching Wally's face for a change   in   expression.   Wally   just shrugged. "Terrific." He said. "Why'd you ask in the first place." "What kind of a friend are you supposed to be?" Georgy grumbled in defeat. "The sane one." Wally shot back.

Later, when he was tinkering with the bell, Georgy was still a little sore about it all. Wally and his ridiculous new found caution and Raff and his stupid remarks on him and Anna. And anyway, he thought grudgingly, it wasn't like he hadn't ever considered kissing Anna. He had just been waiting for the right moment – and that moment hadn't seemed to want to come. Somehow, that thought put another dent in his mood.

He got all the supplies he needed from shop room. With nothing but the dim glow of the emergency signs to light, his way and all that had happened over the course of the previous months, being back at school after dark felt strange. Scarier than before, somehow. Like there could be something dangerous waiting around every corner. That thought alone was enough to make Georgy's hair stand on end and excite him at the same time. The most dangerous part of his plan, however, was still ahead of him. He switched on his flashlight, began rummaging through drawers and cabinets, looking for a welding torch, and hard solder. He clamped the bell hammer in a vice and adjusted the tube that was meant to hold the firecracker to be at an angle. 'Neutral flame.' He thought and switched on the machine.

The flame of the torch seemed incredibly bright in the relative darkness of the room and Georgy briefly worried that someone might see it flashing from the outside, before he pushed the thought away. The shop room was facing the football field, after all, and it was very unlikely that there would be someone there at that hour, save maybe the hobo they assumed lived under the bleachers. Better finish up quick, Georgy thought. Once the metal was glowing cherry-red, he melted the hard solder and filled the gap between the tube and the hammer with it. Satisfied, he switched off the torch but without the roaring hiss of the escaping gasses and the bright light of the flame, it was suddenly very quiet and dark. Georgy closed his eyes and listened. Nothing. He let out a breath he hadn't realized he'd been holding and began putting everything back where he'd found it. Nobody could know that he'd been here.

He held his hand over his construction and, after realizing that it still was far too hot to touch, he picked it up with a set of pliers and held it under some cold water. Then he put it back into his bag, left the room and locked it. Once he had reached the assembly hall where the school bell normally hung, he quickly got to putting everything back together. 48 hours until D-day. The problem was that he couldn't very well test out his contraption, since it would require him to get the bell to ring in the middle of the night. Instead, he simply put a match into the tube and attach it to an empty matchbox. Then, when he came back to check the next night, he would be able to see whether it had burned down without anyone being any the wiser.

"Wake-y, wake-y!" "Get lost, squirt." "Mom said I should go see if you were awake." "Go away, Tony!" Georgy pulled his pillow over his head. His little brother didn't care though. In a matter of seconds, he had switched the light on and pulled up the blinds. Bright light flooded the room and bit Georgy's eyes, as he flung the pillow across the room at Tony. Bullseye! It hit his brother square in the jaw and he landed on his butt. Georgy didn't get to enjoy the moment for long though, Tony was already sucking in a deep breath, his brown eyes centered on George. "Mom!" He squawked. "Mom, George pushed me!" Their mother, in costume jacket and slippers and looking more than a little irritated, stuck her head into the room. "Get up, it's late." She snapped at Georgy and turning to Tony she added: "And you quit yer bellyachin'." "But he threw a pillow at me." Tony pouted but their mom had already disappeared down the hall. "Unless that pillow was filled with bricks, I don't need ta hear about it." She called back from the kitchen. Georgy wormed his way out of bed. He felt like he hadn't slept at all.

Somehow, he still managed to get to school on time. The cold wind whipped through his hair and jump-started his brain. He looked at his watch. If it was working correctly, the bell was due to ring any moment. Georgy locked up his bike and went to loiter around in the assembly hall again, until it finally did and a thin trail of smoke rose from the casing. He quietly congratulated himself on a job well done and went to class in a stellar mood.

It didn't last very long, however, in part because Raff had decided to be a colossal pain in the fanny that morning, but mostly because Anna didn't show at all during recess. Even didn't know where she was, and Georgy only felt a little better after Wally suggested that maybe she was just sick. She didn't come to school the next day or the day after that. Had called the Dasher residence and told them what they had already suspected: Anna wasn't feeling well and resting. "Bad case of the flu?" Wally wondered when Thursday rolled around and there was still no trace of her. Thursday afternoon, Georgy even tried calling her himself but after a very awkward conversation with Arty that only went in circles, he had almost given up. When he told his friends the next morning, Raff looked at him as if he had lost it. "Here's an idea." He said like Georgy was an idiot. "Why don't you just go and check on her yourself, if you're that worried?" Georgy blushed furiously but it was decided. After school, Georgy and Wally hopped on their bikes. They said their goodbyes to Raff who was expected at his grandma's for lunch and raced along the winding road, which led up to Anna's house. Sweating and gasping for air, they arrived at the gate. The mansion was even more impressive during daytime, Georgy thought. He peered through the bars and spotted the black Mercedes on the driveway.

He rang the doorbell and the butler's croaky voice came over the intercom. "Yes?" Not one for small talk, Georgy thought nervously and cleared his throat. "Yes, hello, Mister, er, Arthur." He tried to sound as casual as possible, like he was talking to a friend. When Arty didn't say anything, he went on: "I am George Thomson, that friend of Anna's who was here a week ago? Me and my friend Walter..." He hesitated. Wally gave him a thumbs-up. "We wanted to visit her. See how she is doing?" This time, Arty almost didn't let him finish his sentence. "No." He said simply. "Miss Anna isn't in any state to entertain visitors." "Oh." Georgy said. "What does she have? Is she contagious?" Wally asked. "The flu." Arty said, sounding rather irritated like they should have known better than to ask. "Nasty. Virulent. Now leave." Georgy gave the intercom a funny look. "Tell her to get well soon." Said Wally. "Yeah, we-" Georgy began but the intercom crackled with static and went quiet. The boys stared at each other for a moment. Wally gave a low whistle. Georgy cursed under his breath. "C'mon, let's get out of here." Wally said and had already taken a step toward his bike, when a voice called out to them. "George, Wally, is that you?" They looked up and saw Anna standing at her window. "Anna? Yeah, we're here." Georgy waved with both arms. "Your butler said you're sick and we can't see you. We-" But Anna had already slammed her window shut with enough force to knock over a small vehicle. "What was that?" Asked Wally. "No idea." The intercom came to live again. "Miss Anna has time for you now." More static, then the gate swung open.

When the boys reached the door, Arty had already opened it. "Pardon my earlier rudeness. I appear to have misconstrued the meaning of 'I don't want anyone to see me.'" He said by way of greeting, not at all sounding sorry, his eyes instead resting on Wally's greased hair and patchy leather jacket. Wally waggled his eyebrows at him. "Follow me, if you please." Arty drawled and turned his back on them. Wally was just as impressed by the house as Georgy had been his first time there. "This is crazy." He whispered and Georgy nodded enthusiastically. Arty pretended not to see, as he led them up the staircase and opened the door to Anna's living room. "This way." He said, giving both of them a stern glare "May I suggest, however, not to overstay your welcome?" "Yeah, alright." Georgy grumbled. "Just wanna see how she is, is all."

They had crossed the room in a matter of seconds. Georgy carefully pushed the door to her bedroom open. Only a little light made it through the curtains and bathed the room in a dim glow. Anna was huddled up on her bed, the blanket pulled up over her nose like a cocoon, surrounded by a mountain and a half of comic books. "Hi." Georgy said and Wally nodded in greeting. "How are you?" "Could be worse." Anna said, her voice muffled. She fidgeted under the blanket. The entire situation was weird. "Are you running a fever?" Georgy asked more to bridge the awkwardness than anything else. "No." "Is there... Is there something we can do for you?" "No." Even through the blanket, Anna sounded agitated. Although the room was almost too dark to see, Georgy noticed the furrow in her brow and that she wasn't looking at him. Something was very wrong. And I bet whatever it is, its's hiding under that blanket, he thought. Wally seemed to be thinking the same thing. "You got that thing over your face so you don't breathe on us?" He asked. Anna glowered at him. "Can... Can we see?" Georgy asked carefully. "Your face, I mean." Anna shot him a venomous look then she sighed and let the covers slip into her lap. "Jesus." Wally breathed. "Yeah, some healing magic would come in handy right now." Anna grumbled as she looked at them. "Was that him?" Georgy asked. Anna nodded. In the near darkness of the room, it looked like she had dipped her face into a pool of molten wax that had since congealed into an uneven coat of ridges and hollows. Georgy pulled back the curtains. Anna's face was swollen and bruised, streaked with purples, reds and yellows. "That asshole." Georgy hissed through clenched teeth. "It's fine." Anna said simply. "It's not that bad anymore. And besides." She said with a wavering smile. "Chicks dig scars." "Gotta try harder than that to get a scar." Wally said but something about his voice was off. Georgy just looked at her face in consternation. His ears were ringing. "I refused to go buy him more stuff." Anna told them. "And because he was drunk, I got it." "That's what I thought." Georgy said and took a seat on the edge of Anna's bed. "Did you go to the police?" "No, I didn't. Arty sent him away. Well, hauled him out of the house, tossed him in the car and told the driver to floor it, is more like it. And he telegraphed my mom. She'll be home in two days." "This has to stop." Georgy said. "We gotta do something. Anything. Like, if we... if we could put those dealers out of business, then he'll have to find a new source and... Maybe..." His mouth felt dry. "That doesn't solve the problem. Unless it somehow makes that guy into less of a piece of shit." Wally said and plopped down on a chair next to the bed. Anna sadly shook her head. "Rehab couldn't do it, I don't think we can." There was a short-lived silence. "What about your parents?" "Didn't you just hear the bit about rehab? And my mom lets Lars get away with everything." Wally turned to George. "So." He said nonchalantly. "How are we going to do it?" Georgy thought about it for a moment. It felt like his head was filled with molasses. "Two things." He said slowly. "Gotta stop the people selling and the people delivering." Wally raised his brows at him. Georgy shook his head. Maybe he would be able to think of something later, when he was far, far away from Anna's room. "I'll think of something." He said. "Thanks." Anna smiled. Georgy's gut felt like it was being compressed by a vice. She leaned over and kissed his cheek. Everything after that went by in a blur. They talked for a while and Georgy tried to find out if there was something they didn't know yet, but he couldn't rightly focus. It didn't matter anyway. Anna didn't know if the Frenchman was a French

106

teacher, nor did she know anything about his schedule. A dead end.

It took another week for Anna to come back to school. Sunday evening, she called to tell him they could meet during recess. It felt strange, having his mom ask who he'd been talking to. "Just a friend." He had said, though his ears had been tinted pink by the end of the conversation. Well, she is just a friend, he told himself sourly. What was his problem, anyway?

He had told Anna that he had a little surprise for her, like a welcome-back present. It did, however, require her to be at the assembly hall before the bell rang. The rest of the conversation had mostly been Anna hassling him to him to tell her what the surprise was. Georgy didn't give in to it though, arguing that it wouldn't be a surprise that way.

When Georgy's parents went to visit some friends that evening, he went in the garage and made the powder. Every one of the ingredients had to be finely ground and added in just the right measure. He poured some of the mixture into the matchbox and stuffed the remaining space with cotton balls. All that was left to do was exchange the inner part of it with the one at school. After considering for a bit, he decided to hide the rest of the powder in his room, with the vague notion that it may come in handy at a later time.

Setting up the charge had been child's play but Georgy still felt anxious when he went to bed that night. The match had burned down true to form, sure, but what if the gunpowder ended up not working? Or working too well? Why, oh why, hadn't he tested it beforehand. Georgy pulled the blanket over his head. He couldn't decide what would be worse: Showering the assembly hall with shrapnel or having to tell Anna that the surprise was there not being a surprise at all.

The next morning, he left Tony and his mother to squabble at the kitchen table and was one of the first people to arrive at school. Stealing glances at the bell, he couldn't help but feel guilty. What had happened to not wanting to break anything? Breaking things meant someone had to pay for them.   Nothing to do about it now, he thought, too late for regrets. He felt a little better when Anna, accompanied by Wally entered the building. He waved until they noticed him.

The second they were within earshot of each other, the bell rang. Georgy bit back a smile and ducked his head. Anna planted one on his cheek. He felt his face flush just a little and returned the wide smile that she gave him. "So." She said by way of greeting. "Where's my awesome surprise?" Georgy jerked his thumb over his shoulder. Anna and looked at the wall behind him. Georgy and Wally pretended not to be interested at all, watching the other students when there was a quiet hiss, followed by a bang like somebody had popped a balloon. Some people screamed, some stood frozen in place and Miss Sanders, who had just walked in, jumped a few feet in the air. Some smoke rose from the bell, just enough to be noticeable, not enough to trigger the fire alarm. Georgy grudgingly turned to look. That hadn't been as climactic as he would have liked. Just then, the casing slipped off the bell and hit the floor with a loud clattering sound that seemed all the louder in the stunned silence of the hall. "There we go." Georgy muttered under his breath. A small group of students began to gather around the remains of the bell. "So." Georgy grinned, mimicking Anna's tone from before. "How'd you like your surprise? Guess it will take a while till you have to hear that thing ring again." Anna looked like she had swallowed her tongue. "You remembered? That I said that?" Wally snorted. "As you may have noticed just now, George can't really tell whether people are serious or not. Just keep that in mind when you talk to him. Otherwise things are liable to get crazy." "Better crazy than boring." Anna said; smile bright enough to light up the entire room, the familiar twinkle in her eyes. And Georgy knew that it was because of him.

The door flew open and Mister Woodman came rushing in. He looked absolutely livid. "Out of my way!" He huffed as he pushed past gawking students. "Which of you good-for-nothing little rats was that?" And with a huff like a raging bull he announced what everybody had already been able to tell. "This'll have to be replaced! How's anyone supposed to know when classes start now?" "They have taught us to read clocks, dad." Wally said with an eye roll. Mister Woodman's nostrils flared dangerously. "Don't mouth off to me, boy." He spat and left the hall just as quickly as he'd come, bell case in hand, presumably to inform the principal.

Chapter 6   Walls

A strong wind blew low-hanging clouds across the dark grey sky and heavy rain poured down from above like somebody had opened the floodgates in heaven. April, true to its reputation, had kept everyone on their toes with weeks with thunderstorms and flooded basements and only by the end of it had a gentle breeze announced the coming of May. Because the rain had kept him inside for days on end, Georgy had spent his time reading and daydreaming, imagining how someday he would sail the stormy sea and travel all over the world on a ship, the sun on his face and the wind at his back. Though it was good fun in the beginning, the weather began affecting his mood eventually and then something else happened that made him feel even worse. Philip was due to return to school. After Mister Woodman had almost caught the dealer, things had quieted down around Kevin. As far as they could tell, business wasn't going well and now they were only checking on him from time to time. With Philip coming back, however, there was a chance that would change.

Georgy looked at his watch. Almost three o'clock. He and Raff were going to pay Olly a visit. He got dressed and got on his bike. Raff's bike was already chained to a lamppost outside Olly's house. Georgy rung the doorbell, then raced up the stairs to the third floor where Olly lived. Olly was already waiting for him at the door and with a hand gesture instructed Georgy to be quiet. ”Pop's in one hell of a mood. Sobering up in the living room. Come in.“ Without a sound, they crept through the corridor toward Olly's room. It was absolutely tiny, with barely enough space for a bed and a desk and Raff had once jokingly said that it looked more like a prison cell than anything else. Olly hadn't found that funny at all. It was messy, dirty clothing, shoes and schoolbags littering the floor and paper and magazines stacked all over the place.

Georgy found a spot on the bed that wasn't occupied by an assortment of dirty plates, cups, empty pop cans or Raff, who was now so close to him, that their shoulders were touching. "What's going on?" Georgy asked in a whisper. Olly closed the door. "Somebody reported my dad to the police." He said. "What? Why?" Olly shrugged and ran a hand through his hair. "You know we're building a house in that new residential area." "Yeah, I know. So?" "And on the other side of the street, there is that rich couple. The physicians?" "Those people with the ridiculous last name?" Raff asked. He was playing a game of catch with himself, using a rolled-up pair of Olly's socks. "Yeah, the Brewing-Gotobeds. How do you know them?" "I don't really. My dad does." " So, they went to the police, right? Said that the roof is too tall. That it 'exceeds regulation' by four inches and blocks their view of the landscape when they look out the attic window." "Pish, so what." Raff huffed and ended his game by bouncing his makeshift ball off of Georgy's ear. "Not like there is much to see." "You don't get it." Olly said, wringing his hands in his lap. "They want us to tear down the roof or they'll take us to court." "You're joking." Georgy said in disbelief. "That's ridiculous." Raff muttered, measuring four inches between his fingers. "You can say that again, boy!" Came a muffled voice through the wall and they flinched. Olly's dad appeared to have been listening in. "You know, what I should do? Build a wall in front of that harpy's door, all the way

111

around her house while I'm at it, I should! Like a nice, standard-god-darned issue brick wall, according to all the damned regulation, so she'll know what it means not being able to look out of your window! Regulations!" While Olly's dad went on raging, Olly turned to Georgy, his eyes wide. 'Help.' He mouthed. Georgy scratched his head, thought about it for a moment, and nodded. "That's a good idea, Mister Olly's dad." He called through the wall.

"What's that mean?" The other boys looked at Georgy with something between curiosity and agitation. Georgy grinned. "You heard me. We'll wall them in." "What, how?" "Easy. It's a developmental area, right. They'll have all the supplies we need just lying around. Bricks, cement, wheelbarrows and so on. We'll go there at night and put walls in front of all the doors and windows on the ground floor." "That's insane." Raff said, amazed. "But what if they wake up?" Olly asked. "We'll get in so, so much trouble." "We'll have to do it when they're not home." Georgy said. That was what was going to be hard to figure out. They couldn't very well break into the Brewing-Gotobeds' house and nick their personal planners. To his surprise, Raff perked up at that. "There's a charity ball at the community center on Saturday. Proceeds go to some noble cause or whatever. It's really just for all the big wigs to outdo each other with how much they can donate. I bet the Gotobeds'll be there too." Georgy grinned again. "That way, we'll have enough time to finish the job and they'll even have a surprise waiting for them when they get back home. What do you say, Olly?" Olly was quiet for a moment, then he said: "Well, it won't help my dad but maybe it'll make him happy." "I bet it will."

112

"Don't try to hit on Lisa on Saturday." It was a sunny Monday morning – May had apparently decided that it was summer - and the boys were standing in a corner of the schoolyard in t-shirts and shorts. Olly was even wearing sandals. Georgy had meant to use that day's recess to discuss their plans for the Gotobed's house's renovations, as he'd started referring to it in his head but Wally, who didn't know about that yet seemed to have plans of his own. He was fixing Raff with an all too casual look that clearly indicated that he meant business. Raff snorted. "Why would I be hitting on her – don't exactly make a habit of hanging out with her outside of school." "You don't even really make a habit of hanging out with her in school." Georgy pointed out. "What are you talking about? We're practically best friends. I dig the whole air-head hippy thing." "You would know of air-head, wouldn't you." Wally said with a mild smile but Georgy was sure he saw something flashing in his eyes. "Who is Lisa?" Olly asked. "That blonde girl from Chemlab." Wally replied. "The cute one? Who always wears those really unfortunate outfits?" Raff supplied helpfully. Wally gave him a weird look. "Listen, man." He said very quietly. "I'll be seriously pissed if you hit on her at her birthday party." Raff scoffed. "Well, you won't have to worry about that." He grumbled, sounding distinctly sour. "I didn't even know it was her birthday." "She invite you?" Wally asked, turning to George who shrugged. "Must have missed the postman." "He doesn't need an invite." Said a voice from behind them. "He's my plus one." Anna and rounded the corner.

"Hey." Wally said with a smile. "I was just telling the guys about that party of yours." "Hope you have an awful lot of fun." Raff muttered under his breath. Lisa

113

looked at him for a solid thirty seconds, then she giggled. "I suppose you can come, if you really want. I mean, Urs will be there, too." "Oh, I..." Raff's cheeks were colored a delightful pink within moments. "I mean, that's cool, I guess. Did she.. I mean." He ran a hand through his gelled hair and exhaled a shaky breath.

"Um..." Said Olly, effectively putting an end to Raff's rambling. "Didn't we have... you know... Plans? On Saturday?" The girls gave them suspicious looks. "Oh yeah, right." Georgy said. "Afraid we won't be able to make it on Saturday. We have... uh, things to do, as it were." "Things to do?" Anna echoed and quirked a brow at him. "What kinds of things could those be?" "Er, well, you see..." Georgy stuttered. What they were planning this time wasn't really just a small prank, so he'd rather not tell her in the middle of the schoolyard. Maybe later, he could- "Fine." Anna said with a shrug, stirring him from his thoughts. "Don't tell me, I'll just have to play Lois Lane till I find out." "Does she ever find out?" Olly asked, looking at Anna as if he was just now seeing her for the first time. "Don't you read?" Anna asked back in mock-offense. "Of course she does, she was the first Superwoman, after all. So you may as well spill it all now." She winked.

Olly, not knowing Anna very well and obviously very impressed, judging by his rose tinted cheeks and the wide-eyed look he was giving her, complied almost immediately. Once he had finished his story, the girls looked ready to jump into action. "We'll help." Anna offered. "I'm tired of just being told about the things that you guys get up to. I want to be there." Georgy looked at Raff who shrugged, then looked at Olly, who was still staring at Anna like she had just manifested out of thin air. "Uh, sure, I suppose... Just... What about the party?" "Oh, I don't mind at all. I'll just have the party another time." Lisa said, smiling serenely. "You'll be there, won't you?" She asked, turning to Wally. Wally shrugged and made a face. "Don't really see what the point is – unless we actually plan on getting caught and Olly's dad ends up with more money, 'cause the state pays the time we do." He gave Georgy a hard look at these words and Georgy pretended not to notice. In a flash, he remembered the conversation they had not too long ago, about pranks going too far. This was different, Georgy decided defiantly, the Gotobed had it coming. "It's a statement!" Raff said theatrically. "That just because they're rich they can't just do what they want." "Like a form of non-violent civil protest against capitalism." Lisa said happily. "Exactly." Raff enthusiastically agreed. "What she said." Wally sneered in his general direction. "Sure. And if they don't get it, we'll just start extorting them for protection money." "Why not? Maybe Olly's dad could buy a new roof from that." "You guys are kidding. ...Right?" "Yeah, we're kidding Olly." "So, deal or no deal?" Anna asked, in that business-like tone, completely unfazed by the others. "Deal." Georgy said, though he felt conflicted. Maybe it wasn't a good idea. Having so many people along would make things more complicated. "Cool. Let's just all meet at Lisa's this afternoon. We'll discuss the details there. I'd suggest you come to my place but my parents are home and the general mood is pretty down because of Lars." "No problem." Said Lisa. "I'll get some snacks ready."

Once the girls had left and the boys were on the way back to their classroom, Raff turned to Wally and made a face. "You'll be there, won't you?" He said in a high-pitched voice, perfectly imitated' s tone. "What's up with that?" "What, you sore you're still single?" Wally asked nonchalantly. "Wait, what?" Raff stopped dead in his tracks. "You're with Lisa now?" Wally just shrugged with mischievous grin.

Lisa's folks owned a house on the mountain as well, though it looked nothing like the mansion Anna lived in. It wasn't modern at all but rather looked like a miniature chateau – though 'miniature' was relative. It was white and grey and orange, and Georgy was pretty sure he had seen something like it before. On a postcard, maybe.

Lisa, who didn't fit in with the imposing backdrop at all in her wide green shirt and flowy skirt, was leading them into a large, elegant salon that could have doubled for a ballroom, Georgy felt like he had been transported to a fairytale castle. The furniture looked expensive and all the surfaces were so shiny that he was convinced that they only existed to look nice and nothing else. A large window let him look out at the backyard, which had all the makings of a natural reserve, although those usually didn't look like they were being meticulously maintained by what would have to be a legion of gardeners. They even had a pool – and it wasn't one of the varieties that one usually found in backyards either but big enough to house a small whale and surrounded by sun umbrellas and beach chairs. And on one of those chairs lay Anna baking in the sun.

Lisa led them outside and none of them said a word, all of them much too impressed with their surroundings, except for Wally maybe, who looked rather at ease. Georgy suspected that he had been there before. On a garden table next to Anna, there stood a crystal decanter on a mound of ice in a bowl. It was filled with orange juice. A little while later the boys were standing huddled together, holding on to their cups. Anna had gotten up to greet them. Georgy had that weird feeling again - that feeling of being utterly out of place. He wasn't sure if he would ever get used to it.

"So, what's the plan?", Anna asked. Georgy sniffed and shook off the feeling. "We gotta win ourselves some time." He said. "So we can keep working for as long as possible. They'll probably take the car – everything else wouldn't make much sense, wearing a ball gown and heels and all that." "Got experience with that, do you?" "Shut up. Anyway. You." He pointed at who was handing out pieces of iced cake. "Will go to the community center with Wally. Deflate their tires. That should buy us, what, half an hour, maybe? If we do it too early, somebody might see and tell them about it – then it would be a waste of manpower and they might end up coming home sooner than they would have otherwise." Lisa nodded in understanding and Georgy saw how Wally gave her a searching look. Like he was making sure she knew what she was getting into. He pretended not to see. "Raff, Olly, Anna – we are going to do some manual labor." He said grimly. Anna grinned. "I don't mind getting physical." She said and exaggeratedly waggled her eyebrows. Raff stared at her like she was a mystical creature. Georgy closed his eyes for a moment. Oh boy. He decided to pretend not to be able to hear, either. "Raff and I are going to borrow a wheelbarrow and liberate some bricks. There's a construction site right around the corner. I checked it out after school the other day. That should have everything we need." "So, what, I get to watch you lug heavy stuff around?" Anna asked with a pout. "If you want t-augh." Wally had kicked Raff in the shin before he could finish his sentence. "Not at all." Georgy said, rubbing his nose bridge. "There's a long garden hose..." He glared at Raff who thankfully remained quiet. "...just lying around there. The place already has running water. You're in charge of getting us water for the concrete... And get some tools so we can apply it to the bricks later." "Cool." Anna grinned at him. "I'm sure, we'll have heaps of fun." Said dreamily and threw Wally a kiss. Wally returned the gesture and Raff pretended to gag. Wally threw him a kiss as well. Olly was watching them interestedly. Georgy sighed. Time to wrap this up.

"It'll be fine." He said, mostly to himself, not that anyone was listening anymore anyway. Had pulled Wally over to a beach chair, where they were talking quietly and Raff had busied himself, trying to shove Olly, who was doing his best to fight back, into the pool. Georgy turned to Anna. "The physicians are the only people living on that street by this point. But another thing. What did Philip want from you at school today?" He'd been keeping an eye on the guy all day and especially when Philip had approached Anna. He'd punched out a guy before, he could do it again if he needed to, he was pretty sure. "Bah." Anna rolled her eyes. "Told me that he got some new icky stuff or something, I didn't really get it." "What'd you tell him?" Georgy asked. Anna shrugged and made a face. "I wanted to tell him to shove off, except in not

118

so many words. I just said that Lars isn't home and won't be for the rest of the month."

"Okay, that's good." Georgy nodded thoughtfully, looking at his hands. "But we really need to put an end to that little business that guy has built for himself. I just need a bit more time." "Thanks." He looked up when Anna squeezed his shoulder. "But you don't have to do all that stuff for me." Georgy was confused. "But I haven't done anything yet." He said. Anna shook her head and smiled. "'Course you did. The key, the bell, my brother – I wouldn't call that nothing." She went quiet for a moment, then she added in a low voice. "You know, you don't have to... do all that stuff, to... I don't know, impress me. Even if you didn't, I'd still think you were a..." "What are you whispering about?" Raff called over to them, obviously in a fantastic mood, a sopping-wet Olly looking absolutely miserable behind him. "Wouldn't you like to know?" Anna teased and Raff made a face at her. Georgy didn't say anything. He would have liked to know, as well.

"GEORGE! COME GET THE PHONE RIGHT NOW!" Georgy sighed and went into the living room. Wally, Olly and Raff had all already called that morning. His mother was fuming. "Ye seem ta' be under the impression that I'm yer personal secretary. Next time, use yer own damn legs and pick up yerself because I'm just gonna let it ring." She said when he took the phone from her hands. "And it's a girl, so ya better mind yer manners. Don't give me that look, young man. Ya treat her right or yer father will her bout it." Georgy did the best to cover the receiver with his hand. He gave his mother a grudging nod,

119

exaggerated eye roll and all and she wagged her finger at him before scurrying away. "Hi George, it's Anna." Georgy hoped to god that she hadn't just heard all that. "Hey, what's up?" "Just checking in. We meet at your place, right?" "Uh, no. In front of the church. It's our, uhm, universal meeting spot, so to speak." Georgy could feel himself blushing. In truth, although they did meet in front of the church more often than not, he really just didn't want Anna to see his room. It wasn't a bad room, he thought, it was perfectly adequate. Compared to Anna's room, however, it was sort of pathetic. All the furniture was old and cheap looking. He felt a little guilty, thinking about it that way, especially after what Wally had said a while ago, about giving Anna a chance. He just couldn't help it. "We'll walk to the development area from there." He said with a firm nod to chase away the hang-ups. "Split up into two groups, get acquainted with the area during daytime." "So, like a scouting mission?" "Something like that. After that we'll just have to wait for nightfall." "Sounds awesome. See you there."

The doorbell rang around 04.30. That could only be Raff, Georgy thought, though it still was pretty early and Raff usually took a 'Better late than never' approach to these sorts of things. He could hear voices at the door, his mother probably opened it. Georgy groaned. He was going to hear about that later, wasn't he? The door to his room was pushed open and to his surprise, his mother smiled at him in a way that almost made him uncomfortable. With a strange mixture of bashfulness and pride. "Got yourself a little visitor." She said sweetly.

There he was, sitting at his desk – really an old

kitchen table with the stains and knife-marks to show for it - on a chair that seemed to protest its own existence every time Georgy so much as breathed – and in the doorframe stood Anna. He felt like someone had filled his insides with solid ice, he was that stiff. He could hear his brother shouting. "Georgy and his girlfriend sittin' in a tree-" In the background but his brain barely registered the words. "Holler if you need anything." His mother said and closed the door.

"Uh, why don't you have... a seat!" Georgy blurted as he jumped up from his chair. The wood groaned indignantly. For a few moments, he just stood there awkwardly, then he went to sit on the bed. It was old and smelled kind of funny. It also had belonged to his grandma once. Anna plopped down on the chair, her eyes trailing across the walls, the green curtain which clashed terribly with the flowery wallpaper and which hid his clothes and the poster of a sailing ship above his head. "So this is where it all goes down. Hi, by the way." Georgy gave her an awkward wave. "Is this the desk you sit at when you think of all those crazy ideas? D'you think I'll think of something clever if I touch it?" "I'm not sure if-" She shook her head. "I'm just messing." They were quiet for a moment. Georgy's mind was blank, save for one thought that seemed to be on endless repeat. 'This is not how this day was supposed to go.' Anna had gotten up again and was inspecting the built-in shelve and the collection of loose drawers, which housed his books and a few small model ships. "Sure got a lot of those." She said running a finger along the cover of *The Sea-Wolf.* "179" he mumbled. "You built those yourself?" She asked and carefully took a white model ship off its stand. Hope she doesn't find that childish, Georgy thought as he got up and stood next to

121

her. "Yeah, I did." He said. Her hair sure smelled nice. He shook his head. Anna chuckled. "What now, you did or you didn't? Don't lie, I can't stand people taking credit for the hard work of others." "Yeah, I did. It's the USCGC Eagle." "You know, I'm getting the sense that you really like ships." She said with a soft smile. "I do." He said. "I'll sail on that one, one day, when I join the navy." "Planned that far ahead, have you." "I've known since I was eight. Secure job, decent pay and I'll get to see the world." "And you'll have a lass and a brat in every port?" She mumbled absentmindedly. "No." Georgy said, a little offended but Anna didn't seem to notice. "I have no idea what I'll do once I'm done with school." She said and put the model back on its stand. "My dad made a deposit for me. For college and whatever comes after, but..." She trailed off. "Why not start your own comic series?" Georgy said. "You're really into those." "Sure. But I can't even draw."

"Are ye kids hungry? How about some sandwiches?", Georgy's mother had come in and without waiting for a reply, she deposited a large platter with more on it than two people could realistically eat in an afternoon. "No." Georgy was just about to say, glaring daggers at his mom but Anna interrupted him. "Awesome, thanks." Anna said and immediately grabbed a sandwich. "Just dig in, girl. Put some meat on your bones." Georgy's mother said with a nod. "Yes, please do." Georgy said more quietly, so only Anna could hear. "We'll be eating those for the rest of the week otherwise." Anna laughed through a mouth of ham and bread as Georgy's mother left the room. About five minutes later, she came back with Raff in tow, who made a big show of covering his eyes when he entered. "What's up folks, are you decent? Should

I leave?" "Very funny." Georgy hissed but Anna was already one-step ahead. "Did you hear from Urs lately?" She asked nonchalantly as Raff blushed. "Uhh, err, Urs? Did she... Say... Things? About calling me?" "Didn't she tell you?" Anna asked innocently. "Tell me what?" Raff asked back, a desperate quality to his voice. Georgy had to suppress his laughter. "Oh, you don't know? Well, never mind then." "What did she... What did she..." Georgy wished he had camera at hand. The expression on Raff's face was priceless and it was a shame that it wouldn't be preserved for future generations to see. "My bad, I guess." Anna winked. "Forget I said anything." Georgy burst out laughing. Now he really wished he had a camera.

Their little 'scouting mission' as Anna had called it, didn't turn up anything particularly useful. It was a construction site, after all and all the things they need were in ample supply. Still, Georgy thought, getting acquainted with the premises while they still had time couldn't hurt. Plus Anna had sat on his luggage rack the entire way there, which had been nice.

Raff had suggested they hunker down in the upstairs of the unfinished house of Olly's parents. Had brought some muffins, which they munched away at while waiting for the Gotobed's to finally leave. They took turns watching the front door until around a quarter to eight when it swung open and Ms. Gotobed waltzed across the threshold like it had insulted her mother. Raff made some rude comment about how he'd rather look out the attic window as well if the only other option was looking at that. Georgy shushed him, though he silently agreed. "Time to get

123

moving." He whispered. "It'll be dark in an hour. We'll start 'round back, just in case someone passes by." Raff, who had been put in charge of operating the wheelbarrow, kept carting over more bricks and they worked, huffing and puffing, mixing concrete and raising their little walls in front of all the doors and windows. It was hard work – there were more than a few scrapes, bruised thumbs and Olly managed to completely ruin his shirt with concrete but they still had so much fun that Georgy had to constantly remind to be quiet. Around 11:30 they were done. Sure – they wouldn't become contractors any time soon, there were more than a few gaps and irregularities in their walls but they had done what they had set out to do: The Gotobed's would have to climb into their house through the attic window that night. They put everything back where they had gotten it, newly erected brick walls excluded and Georgy felt a sense of pride when he looked at their handiwork. "You happy, you slave driver?" Raff asked as he pushed the wheelbarrow, which was currently occupied by Anna back to where it came from. "Enough complaining and put your back into it!" Anna said grinning. Her cheeks were flushed and her hair a mess. Georgy was glad she had had such a good   time.

Once they had deemed everything clean enough, they went back to the house Olly would soon live in. The dim glow of a flashlight illuminated the room they had already waited in before.

"Didn't take as long as I thought it would." Raff said, brushing sweat-slicked hair from his eyes. "Not sure my arms will ever be the same, though." "Think of it as having gotten a high intensity workout." Anna grinned at him from where she sat on the floor. "You can say that again. You're heavier than you look, you know?" "I resent that." "Now we just have to wait for the Gotobeds to come home." Georgy said happily. "Don't even have to mess with their car." "I wish it were brighter down there." Olly said, fidgeting where he sat. "I really want to see the look on that harpy's face when she gets out of her fancy car." "Got a camera." Anna said, though she didn't look convinced. "Maybe we could snap a few pictures, what do you think?" "What, do you want prove in case the police doesn't believe it was you?" Wally asked. Lisa was sitting in his lap. "More like proof that I did a cool thing." She said with a shrug. "Or helped do one, at any rate." "Maybe." Georgy said. "But it won't work without a flash so... I guess I could take a picture from down the street and make a run for it? Meet you guys here once everything has quieted down a bit."

The others mumbled their agreement. "Do you know where you are going to sleep tonight?" Anna asked. "What did you tell your parents?" "Some story about how George, Olly and I'll sleep at Wally's and that Wally'll sleep at my place. Should be fine, as long as our parents don't run into each other or something." Raff said. "So..." Anna looked at him questioningly. Raff pointed over his shoulder at a bundle of cloth on the floor. "We brought our sleeping bags." "You got a place to sleep?" Wally asked. "Anna's place." She said simply. "Her parents aren't home so it doesn't matter when we get back." "What's Arty got to say to that?" Georgy asked but Anna made dismissive gesture. "Caught him sneaking into my dad's Cognac the other day and smoking his cigars. So he won't talk." Anna laughed. "You know what? You'll just all crash at my place. We got a bunch of guestrooms that don't nearly get enough use. It's warmer and you'll get a nice breakfast, too." Georgy felt like Anna was smiling at him in the near darkness of the room. He felt a strange tingling sensation in the pit of his stomach. "Forget breakfast, how about a late dinner?" Raff said, rubbing his stomach for emphasis. "I'm starving."

There was a noise outside and everybody went quiet all at once. The sputtering of a running engine. Wally was the first to respond. "Lights off!" He hissed in a voice that left no room for protest. Raff, George and Anna crept over to the window. "Oh damn." Raff whispered, immediately ducking his head. All the color drained from their faces when the car slowed and came to a stop. "It's the cops." "What are they doing here?" Anna asked a quiver in her voice. Olly, his back pressed into a corner gave a low whimper. "No idea." Said Georgy, his mind reeling with escape-plans and excuses one more ludicrous than the other, before it focused on the immediate. "Away from the window. Move or they'll see us." He gave Anna a shove without really meaning to, but she didn't complain. This was bad. Very, very slowly Raff lifted his head above the windowsill. "I think this is it." informed Wally in the meantime. She sounded composed but her hands were shaking. "What's the sentence for vandalism?" "Easy now." Wally said. "We're not there yet." "What are they doing?" Georgy asked. Raff was squinting down at the street, his nose almost touching the windowsill. "Stopped the car." - "Shit, one of them's getting out. He's coming. Damn, he's coming over here!" The words couldn't have had more of an effect if Raff had shouted them. The room was so quiet that one could have heard the proverbial needle drop. Georgy's mind went blank. They were trapped. Why, oh why hadn't he looked for a way out of the house? He couldn't be caught – that wasn't how it worked. "What's he doing now?" Anna asked tensely. "Don't know." Raff's voice was barely a whisper. "He's standing by the wheelbarrow we used earlier – he..." For a moment, it looked like Raff was at a loss for words. "I think... He's peeing. He's taking a piss in your wheelbarrow." "Are you joking?" Anna sounded so incredulous, it could have been funny. That moment it wasn't. "No." Raff said, still wide-eyed staring down at the street.

"He's finishing up. - Going to the car. - Getting in." They could hear the door close and the engine rev up.

"That was close, wasn't it?" Lisa sighed and let her head roll back against Wally. "No it wasn't." Wally said, looking Georgy square in the eye. "But it could have been." Georgy turned his head away. The feeling of panic in the pit of his stomach had already subsided. "Nobody forced you to be here, you know." Wally snorted. "Guess not." "Speaking of close." Raff said. "You okay there, Olly? You look like you're about to do what that guy down there just did."

It took until just after midnight for the Gotobeds to finally come home. Wally and Georgy hadn't said a word to each other the entire time. What Georgy had done was deposit his bike on an adjacent street, have to run across the construction site to reach it once he had taken the pictures, then he had positioned

127

himself behind the half-finished house next to the Gotobed's so he'd be able to get a good shot.

The car rolled onto the driveway. Somebody turned off the engine and the lights flickered on when Mister and Misses Gotobed opened their doors. Don't seem to have noticed anything yet, Georgy thought, watching the two of them approach the front door. "What on god's green earth is that?!" Mister Gotobed screamed. There was a low thud and a grunt indicating that the man had thrown himself into the wall. "Lola, do you see this? Do you actually see this?!" "The windows!" The woman shrieked. "There are walls in front of all the windows!" The flash of the camera tore through the darkness like a rock through a cobweb and the Gotobeds whirled around. For a split second, Georgy could see their faces and their expressions made his heart skip. They looked absolutely murderous. He started running before the camera finished printing the picture, heart hammering away and laughter bubbling in his chest. "Vandals and hooligans!" Mister Gotobed raved behind him, giving chase. "They should string you all up!"
Deviating from their original plan, his friends had decided to meet on the road leading up to the highway – and Georgy paddled like a madman all the way there. In insight, he didn't know why he had hurried so much. Mister Gotobed had run out of breath after a hundred feet and the others had to wait for an opportunity to slip away unnoticed.

"That guy probably gave himself an ulcer, the way he was screaming!" Raff told Georgy when they caught up with him. "Could even hear him from the other side of the house!" "Good thing that they don't have neighbors yet, they would have called police!" Olly said with a laugh, his hands flying off the handlebars of his bike and into the air in triumph. Now that the danger had passed, his face had some color again. "Especially because his wife was berating him the entire time." Anna said. She had hitched a ride with Raff and looked like she was having the time of her life. "Then it would have been them being reported for noise pollution." Georgy noticed that Wally had been quiet all throughout the conversation. He ignored it.

A little later, they were sitting on the floor in Anna's room telling each other what had happened over and over again, sans Wally and Lisa who had already turned in. Anna had been right, Arty hadn't said a word. He'd quirked a brow at them, covered in concrete dust and dirt as they'd been but when Anna had mimed taking a drag of an invisible cigar he had let them in without question. "And please fix us up something to eat." She had added as they made their way up the stairs.

It was around two in the morning when Olly gave a yawn wide enough to swallow an entire sandwich that they decided to go to bed. "There are two guest rooms down the hall." Anna said. "Each of you can just pick one." "Last time I counted there were three of us." Raff said and stretched. "Not that we mind sharing." Georgy added quickly. Seriously, the nerve of that guy sometimes. "Oh, you can just sleep here." Anna said and gave him a smile. "I don't think there are enough beds with fresh sheets on them anyway and I'd rather not wake the maid..." She trailed off. Georgy glanced over at the couch. It figured.

Of course, he'd get stuck with second best. Now that she'd seen the way he lived, she probably thought he'd find pigsty agreeable. So much for giving people chances. What did Wally know anyway? "Sure, no problem." He said, trying to swallow a sudden surge of anger.

Once the other two had left and Anna had locked herself in the bathroom, Georgy turned off the lights and got on the couch. There wasn't even a blanket. Maybe he should go downstairs and get his jacket? Nah, he'd probably end up running into Arty and that would just be awkward. The door to the bathroom opened and Georgy instinctively closed his eyes. He could hear that Anna wasn't moving. Instead she just stood there, completely still for a moment. Then she sighed and walked over to him; he could feel the hem of what was probably a nightdress brush against his arm. "Don't know what I was thinking." She mumbled. "You're not that kind of guy." Georgy felt a gust of air smelled her shampoo and felt her long hair trail across his face and neck before her lips touched his cheek. "Good night." She whispered and her steps retreated.

Georgy lay awake for a long time, his hand hovering where she had kissed him and it began to dawn on him that he was an idiot.

Breakfast the next morning was a sight to behold. Freshly squeezed orange juice, pancakes, bacon and eggs and even waffles that didn't come out of the deep freeze. Wally and Lisa were missing again but Raff had said that it was their own fault if they were missing out – or maybe Georgy had imagined that. "Got an idea what we could do with the

130

picture." Anna said. "What is it?" Raff asked shoveling bacon onto his plate. "Send them to the local newspaper, you know? Like 'Can't go inside, can't go to bed.' Something like that." "You sure that is a good idea?" Olly asked, looking nervous again. "What if they somehow find out it was us?" "That's not gonna happen." Georgy said. "There's no way they'll catch us by this point."

Anna drove him home because she wanted to take a few more pictures on the way there. She'd parked the car on an adjacent street and they had snuck back into Olly's house. They had a great view of the Gotobeds' porch from the attic window, where Mister Gotobed was trying his darndest to break through the wall in front of the door with a hammer and chisel.

A few days later there was an article in the newspaper entitled *lost your keys, Doc?* With the photographs printed underneath. The article was funny enough, Georgy supposed but somehow he didn't feel as accomplished as he usually did when he pulled off one of is bigger pranks. Only when Olly ran up to him on Monday, telling him that the Gotobeds had dropped all charges because they couldn't afford taking his dad to court anymore since they had to pay someone to dig out their door, did he feel a grim sense of satisfaction.

Chapter 7   Vanishing stag

"Yo Tombstone, you loser." It was the Monday morning after the walls incident and Philip was apparently fixing to make up for lost time – why else would he have been at school that early? He made a beeline toward Georgy the moment he entered the classroom. "Heard you've been hanging around the Dasher-chick. Hoping for table scraps?" Georgy had felt listless since he'd gotten up. "Beat it." He said. "You know, like all the girls do when they see your ugly mug." "Watch your mouth." Philip hissed. "Wouldn't want me to knock the teeth out of it." Georgy glanced at the door Philip had left open. The corridor was still relatively empty – even Wally wasn't there yet. Georgy felt a sudden rush of anger. "Go right ahead." He spat. "It's the only thing you're good at, after all." Philip raised a brow at him. "You know, I could tell you things about that chick'd make you see what a moron you are." "Takes one to know one."   "What's that supposed to mean?" Philip was coming ever closer and Georgy slowly got up from his chair. "That it's only right for a king to know about his subjects." "You just don't know when to shut up, do you Tombstone?" "Make me." Philip launched himself toward Georgy who vaulted across the table. The boys began circling it like angry lions. Philip kept trying to grab Georgy from the other side but Georgy was fast enough to evade him. "Too short for your weight, huh?" Georgy scoffed, sidestepping a meaty arm. "That's all muscle, stick man. You think Dasher digs your scrawny butt?" "More than she does yours, anyway." Philip narrowed his eyes at him. "Really, 'cause I got an invite for Saturday says otherwise. At the town hall. My old man donated a painting, you know? Got a

132

celebration in our honor." "Good for you." Georgy hissed. "Your dad ever donate anything, Tombstone?" Philip asked with a sneer. "What's he do again, fix cars? Maybe he's got some waste oil to spare. If he were important enough to show his dumb foreign face at all." "Important like you?" Georgy shot back. "What, so the bigwigs can rest assured that the taxes they pay for prisons will be put to good use in the future?" "You wanna help me find out?" Philip growled a dangerous glint in his eyes that Georgy had never seen before. Throwing caution to the wind, Philip threw his entire weight at the table, knocking Georgy in the thighs. Georgy hissed in pain and surprise as he stumbled forward, bracing himself against the tabletop with a resounding smacking noise when his palms hit the plastic. He didn't even have time to catch his breath, before Philip grabbed him by the collar and yanked him forward but he wasn't about to go down without a fight. "What the hell is wrong with you two?" Both of them froze. Wally was standing in the door an unreadable expression on his face. Georgy didn't know how long he'd been standing there. "Like, what are you trying to do? Outshine each other with the dumb garbage you say?" "You think I can't take on the both of you at once, Woodchuck?" Philip sneered but Georgy felt the grip on his collar loosen. Wally was just about to say something, when Mrs. Sanders stuck her head over his shoulder. "Good morning, boys. May I please come in?" Wally moved aside. Philip let go of George. "Watch yourself, Tombstone." He whispered. "Or you'll regret it." Georgy heard the blood rushing through his ears, his hands shaking with adrenaline. He racked his brain for some biting retort but the anger seemed to have driven any coherent thought from his mind. The three of them sat down in their usual spots and no one said a word until class started.

When Georgy opened the newspaper that afternoon, his mood got even worse when he saw proof for what Philip had said earlier. The headline read: *Prettying up the city, one-step at a time – Benevolent benefactors donate another beautiful painting to town hall!* He skimmed the article and made a face. *As per tradition and in the spirit of patriotic restoration, another one of the citizens of our fine town donated a priceless work of art this year. The beneficiary, this time, is our very own mayor who will no doubt be delighted with this change of scenery in his conference hall, all thanks to the generous heart and hand of factory owner and town council member, Conrad Shyttles. The painting, a remarkably expressive rendition of a bellowing stag, will be delivered to the town hall this Saturday, and will be officially revealed on Sunday – after church, of course!*

The article went on and on about how a wall in the conference room had even been painted to match the painting's color scheme and how all those who *sadly* wouldn't be able to be there on Sunday would hopefully find *some consolation* in being able to come look at it after the *exclusive showing* that weekend. Yuck.

Under the article, there was a photograph of the painting, framed by a man on either side, one of them the mayor and one of them Conrad Shyttles himself. It was uncanny how much his son looked like him.

Georgy felt something strange, something that he couldn't quite place. Anger, maybe, at how profoundly unfair it all was - That Philip was such a turd and still had everything. That he got to hang out with Anna. After what he'd done. Something had to be done about him, Georgy decided, and he would be the one to do it.

"Open your books on page 34. I hope you people remember more about resonance than you did magnetism. I'd hate to have to fail you all. Or have you in my make-up course this summer." Nobody particularly liked physics class. Georgy thought it was okay, although Mister Rampart, the teacher, had the reputation of being a total hard ass. "Can anyone tell me what an ampere balance is?" Mister Rampart asked, looking around the class. No one said anything. Mister Rampart gave a frustrated huff. "Does the name 'Thomson' ring any bells?" "No. But I hear there are other things that he does to them." Georgy froze in place and blushed a furious crimson. Mister Rampart rolled his eyes. "Just once, Philip, and I know it is asking much, I would like you to contribute something useful to class." "Whatever you say, teach." Philip said snidely, reclining in his chair. That moment Georgy wanted to do nothing more than to wipe that shit-eating grin of Philip's face any way he could. At the same time, he didn't want Philip to know how wound-up he still was from that morning.

Georgy   took   a   deep   breath.
To   no   avail.
Maybe Philip knew something he shouldn't, maybe he
didn't - but what had been panic seconds before, now
rose like hot, angry bile in Georgy's throat. The straw
that broke the camel's back. Philip was going to pay.
"George?" Georgy flinched when he heard his
name. "What?" Mister Rampart threw his hands up in
exasperation. "Am I talking to myself here?" "Did you
say something, teach?" Some people giggled at
that. "Quiet Philip. Answer the question, George." "Uh,
sorry. What was the question?"

The idea came to him a couple days later, on his way
home. Anna had told him that she would rather
pound nails into her own forehead than go to that
stupid event at the town hall that weekend. The effect
would likely be the same as being exposed to the
Shyttles for an hour or two, or so she thought and
that had made Georgy's day. As he rode his bike past
the forest edge, no stag in sight, he had to stop for a
moment because he was laughing so hard. What if
when they revealed the painting on Sunday, the stag
was gone?

Once he'd arrived home – nobody else was there as
per usual, his mom and dad were at work and his
little brother at some after-school club – he got a
white bedsheet from the closet in his parents'
bedroom. He went into the living room, spread the
sheet out on the floor, scrounged around his brother's

136

room for the watercolors and got to work.

Anna came to them during recess, as she tended to do as of late even if it meant sending her other friends to lunch by themselves. She had suggested Georgy, Raff, Olly and Wally come along but her friends insisted on going to that little Bistro/Catering place the principal's brother owned and that was just miles out of Georgy's price-range. Without any preamble, she turned to Raff. "I'm sorry but I can't just sit idly by any longer." "Uh, what?" Raff asked, giving Georgy a confused look. Georgy shrugged. "What do you think is going on between you and Urs?" Raff's face fell. "Geez Anna, are you trying to ruin my mood? Nothing's going on. Urs treats me like I got a pox or something." Anna rolled her eyes. "All right." She said. "Listen closely because I'm only going to say this once: Urs thinks you're cute." At those words, Raff's mouth fell open and he seemed to grow a few inches taller in the span of seconds. A wide, absent-minded grin spread across his face. "Really?" He breathed. "But why... Why does she act that way when I try to talk to her?" "Well maybe if you *talked to her* like a human being instead of making vague insinuations and hitting her with the smarm brow..." Wally mumbled. Lisa gave him a kiss. "How about..." She began with a smile. "You put that theory to the test at my party this Saturday?" "You think? But what would I even say?" Georgy felt like somebody had dipped him headfirst into ice water. He'd completely forgotten about the party. It seemed like Lisa somehow was able to smell it, too. "You'll be there too, George, won't you?" Out of the corner of his eye, he could see Wally raise his brows when he hesitated. "Uh, sure. Just... Maybe a little later? When's it start again?" Anny gave him a look that made him squirm in discomfort. It felt like her eyes were drilling their way past his skull and into his brain. "And here I had hoped..." She began gravely and Georgy's heart skipped a beat. "That I'd finally met a guy who's attention span exceeded that of a goldfish. More's the pity." She gave Georgy her best pout and he rolled his eyes. "You're lucky I like you." He mumbled sullenly. "Ditto." Anna said with a laugh, cuffing his shoulder. "Party starts at four." Wally interrupted them. "That a problem for you?" Wally's eyebrows had migrated almost all the way up to his hairline.

He wouldn't tell them, not this time. "Four's too early for me. Do you have an idea how long the party's gonna last?" "We'll have it outside." Lisa said. "In the yard, at the pool, although I believe it said so on the invite." "Goldfish." Anna whispered in a singsong voice. "Then we'll have a barbecue, so I guess... Until nine, at least?" "Yeah, about that." Raff rejoined. "Are we going to have real food or will I have to smuggle in some steak in my shorts?" "What do you mean 'real food'?" Lisa asked with a curious expression. "I'll get there as soon as I can." Georgy cut in. He didn't fancy the conversation devolving into a lifestyle debate and neither did he want to think about eating anything that Raff had carried around under his clothes at any point in time. "My mom's decided that it's time to get our flat into shape and I've been pressganged into the cleaning crew." Nobody questioned that. Raff mumbled a few words of sympathy and Lisa said something about how wars were never just. Georgy nodded his agreement.

Georgy spent half of that Saturday killing time in the general vicinity of town hall, waiting for things to pick up. Around eleven two cars pulled up on the driveway. One looked like a delivery truck and had a rickety sign on top that read 'Henry and sons, painters and scaffolders'; the other was sleek, green and expensive-looking. The painters immediately began unloading their vehicle. Brushes, paint rollers, duct tape and buckets upon buckets of paint were being carried across the parking lot and into the building, where another man had come to open the door. A rotund man dressed like a prospector got out of the other car. He brushed down his jacket and took a moment to watch the painters at work, looking only mildly interested then he slowly made his way over to his trunk. He unlocked it, bent down and with what Georgy disgustedly recognized as a flourish of his hand – as if he were putting on a show - he pulled out a slim rectangular package meticulously wrapped in brown paper.

After Mister Shyttles had dropped off the painting, he got back into his car and drove off without so much as a single look over his shoulder.

Georgy waited another five minutes in case the painters forgot something, then he casually strolled over to the building, just as if he were admiring the architecture. That was the story he would go with, in case they caught him, that he had just wanted to see the place from the inside for a paper he had to write – or something to that effect. He froze for a moment when the wooden gate groaned as it fell shut behind him.

He had to admit, it was impressive, all high ceilings and ornate stonework, that made his footfalls sound unnaturally loud. The conference room was in the upstairs, which meant that that was where the painters were as well. Georgy had decided that he was going to find himself a quiet place, have a sit-down and simply wait for them to leave as though he were meant to be there. He decided on a spot between two pillars in a secluded corridor, pulled a book from his backpack and began to read.

It took until around three when he'd just gotten to the last chapter detailing the exploits of James Cook, that the painters finally left. Georgy smiled to himself and finished the book. Before he decided to get to work, he listened for a moment. Everything was quiet. He snuck down the corridor toward the conference room, quietly praying that it wouldn't be locked. He turned the doorknob and – it was open! Relieved, he slipped inside. Why would they lock the door anyway? Not like people who weren't meant to be there usually got in, in the first place.

In the middle of the room there stood an imposing table, made from polished wood and surrounded by a great deal of chairs. Between the windows with their white frames hung a collection of photographs of previous mayors, along with a few presidents. Three of the walls were white; one was newly mint-green. The entire room smelled of paint and Georgy silentlyy resolved not to linger. There was a wooden contraption with a black curtain blocking the view of most of the green wall and Georgy suspected that the painting was hidden behind it. He pulled on the attached cord and the curtain slid open, revealing the 'Bellowing Stag' in all its glory. Georgy couldn't help but snigger. No wonder, he thought, that Mister Shyttles wanted to get rid of it. The thing was supremely ugly.

Georgy took it off the hook and made to set it down when he heard the front gate swing open with a squeak and a groan. Panic rose in his gut. Not this again, he thought feverishly, sweat already beading his forehead. He quickly shoved the painting back onto the wall, dove for his rucksack and was half-way to the door already, when he realized it was too late. He could hear footsteps approaching. Hoping for the best, he scrambled to get under the table.

141

"Ah, and here we are." Someone said as door swung open. "Feast your eyes on this, Mister Mayor. I hope it is to your liking." "Yes, yes, quite well done, Henry. Quite well done." Georgy couldn't help but raise his brows. Maybe the Mayor was as crazy as his dad said he was, whenever he read local news in the papers. Nobody could possibly find that painting nice to look at. Just then, the mayor sniffed and added: "You chose the perfect color. Shame it has to take the backseat to that hideous waste of canvas." "Of, course, Mister Mayor. Gotta do your duty as a citizen and all that." "At any rate..." The curtain slid shut. "I have to run, Henry. I have an appointment at the middle school – a photoshoot in preparation of the culture fare, you understand." "Sure." Mister Henry said. "You do what you gotta." "And for me that just happens to be playing nice with all the children twice a year." Although he couldn't see the mayors face, George could hear the frustration in his voice. "I don't know, Mister Mayor, my kids love that thing." Said Mister Henry. Georgy quietly prayed that the two of them would just shut up and leave. They mayor sighed. "Yeah, yeah, good idea and all but I'm telling you- If Frenchies didn't do the catering I wouldn't bother. Anyway..." Their footsteps were receding. His heart pounding in his throat, Georgy heard the two men close the door behind them.

He closed his eyes and sucked in a couple deep breaths. If he kept having close encounters like that, he'd   die   at   thirty.

In   prison.
Glancing at his watch, he determined it was a quarter
to five, which meant that if he hurried, maybe he'd
still be able to take a dip in the pool at Lisa's place
and maybe even see Anna in her bathing- No. One
thing   at   a   time.
In the corridor, he had noticed a massive bookcase.
With all the strength he could muster, he shifted it
away from the wall. Perfect place to stash the painting
for the time being. Now all that was left was to get the
bedsheet out of his backpack and pin it to the wall.

Once he was done, he quietly snuck back to the
entrance, only to find that it was locked. Of course,
he thought when his breath caught in his throat,
what exactly did I expect anyway? He rubbed at his
temples in an effort not to panic, then his eyes landed
on the sign that pointed toward the restrooms. It was
worth a shot. The windows lead out to the courtyard,
which probably was even better than making a break
for it through the main door because nobody would
see him there. The problem was that they were on the
second floor. Georgy sniffed, shrugged to himself and
dropped the bag back. Between jumping and
spending the night between dusty bookshelves and
city records, jumping won by a massive margin. He
sat on the windowsill, legs dangling over the edge and
glanced at the gravel underneath. Then he pushed
himself off. He felt the impact all the way up to his
knees and almost slipped on the gravel, his ankle

twisting painfully but he thought when he limped back to the parking lot that had been worth it.

A few minutes later, he was back on his bike and on route to Lisa's party, grinning all the way there.

"Hi Georgy!" She called out dreamily when she saw him. The backyard was littered with brightly colored blankets and equally colorful streamers. He almost asked whether they were biodegradable but thought better of it. Instead, he awkwardly stuck out his hand and mumbled a belated 'Happy Birthday'. "Sorry, I don't have a gift. I wasn't sure whether you-" "'Expected one' was what he'd meant to say but he cut himself off again. Lisa didn't seem to notice. She took him by the arm and led him toward the barbeque. "Don't worry." She said. "You brought yourself. That's enough." "Uhu." Georgy muttered as he looked around. There were people all over the place and out of the corner of his eye; he spotted Wally strumming away on his guitar, surrounded by a group of kids Georgy had never seen before. He was pretty sure that Raff would never have let him live it down but he couldn't see him anywhere. Then he noticed Anna coming toward him. She looked very pretty in her brown dress and- Were those flowers in her hair?

"There you are!" She began without any preamble. "What kept you so long?" "Cleaning and stuff." He mumbled and held his hands out to her as though it proved something. Anna shrugged. "Well, if you say so. I'm glad that you're here, at any rate." Georgy liked the way she looked at him when she said that. "Would you like something to drink?" She asked, tugging on his sleeve. "Gotta hurry though, I'm pretty sure some of Lisa's wackier friends are spiking the punch as we speak." "Uh, sure." He said as he followed her across the lawn. She was still holding on to his sleeve – yet nobody had felt the need to loudly comment on it yet. Where was Raff? "Uhm, Anna?" "Yeah?" "Lisa did invite Raff, didn't she?" "What." She grinned when she poured him a glass of punch. "You think she was messing with him for being a loud-mouthed windbag when she said he could come?" Georgy didn't know what to say to that. When Anna saw his face, she just laughed and pointed over her shoulder. In the shade of a tree, on a blanket all by themselves sat Raff and Urs. Urs seemed to be telling a story or something while Raff stared at her completely enraptured. Georgy snorted when Urs pointed at the table with the drinks and Raff almost fell over his own feet, trying to get there as quickly as possible. "Good for him. Anything new with you?" He asked, turning to Anna. She shrugged. "Nothing much. Other than..." She made a roundabout gesture and sighed. "Yeah?" "Eh, you know. Philip's been doggin' me everywhere I go. Not really sure what he thinks will come of it either. I mean, how am I gonna get the stuff to Lars by this point? Carrier Pigeon?" She laughed but it sounded fake and tired. When Georgy didn't even crack a smile, her face fell a little and she turned away. He immediately felt guilty. "Anyway..." She continued dryly. "When I told him that Lars wouldn't need anything anymore, he outright asked me whether I wanted to buy some for myself. With a beginner's discount because he was going to have a surplus of supply soon... So I stole his lunchbox." Georgy almost choked on his punch. Gasping, he looked at Anna through watering eyes and quickly hid a growing grin behind the rim of his glass. Anna seemed to have noticed though and she was blushing furiously. "Oh, don't laugh." She muttered under her breath. "I just didn't know what else to do. And he left it there unattended so..." "So you didn't even steal it so much as just pick it up?" That moment, strangely, Georgy suddenly felt the overwhelming urge to kiss Anna right there and then. She had to be the most adorable human being he had ever met, the way she looked all bashful all of a sudden, her face a brilliant shade of red, yet her eyes still twinkled. "Don't judge me." She said. "We all have to start somewhere." "Sure." He said grinning. "I mean, he could definitely stand to lose a few pounds. So you basically helped him." He burst into laughter at the face she made at that and she punched him in the arm so hard that he spilled punch all over himself. Once she had gotten him, some napkins he had finally managed to get over how funny it was. "Anyway." She said as he tried in vain to pat dry his shirt. "He's probably gonna fill up on hors d'oeuvre tomorrow, so it's not like it's gonna do him any good in the long run." "You could try 'stealing' them, too." Georgy quipped happily. Anna

146

rolled her eyes but she was smiling. "I think I'll keep it small for the time being. Might put you out of business otherwise." She paused for a moment and gave him a suspicious glance. "You're not gonna try and steal the food for the painting reveal now, are you? It's probably going to be the only good thing there." "Wouldn't dream of it." He said and gave her the most innocent smile he could muster. Anna just raised her brows at him. "I'm serious." She said, jabbing a finger in his general direction. "I'll be bored out of my mind already, I don't want to have to starve, too." "Oh c'mon." He said patting her on the shoulder. "I'm sure you'll have a blast. Just heaps of fun." "Maybe there was something in the punch after all." She said and made to smell his glass, as if to check it for alcohol. "Hey, I'm just saying you should keep an open mind." He grinned. "But how about we go over to the barbecue for a bit? Otherwise I might be the one to starve – I mean, I've been hard at work all day."

Georgy woke up early on Monday, earlier than anyone else in the apartment did. Trying to make sure that it stayed that way, he tiptoed through the hallway and downstairs. The paperboy had already been there, and his heart skipped a beat when he saw the newspaper sticking out of the mailbox. He pulled it out and snuck back into his room.

Vanishing stag – The curious case of the magically disappearing painting: This Sunday morning our local town hall saw a veritable scandal. An expensive painting, donated by our very own Conrad Shyttles, sausage manufacturer and town council member, appears to have vanished into thin air. At the celebration for its reveal, attended by the most outstanding members of our community, the crowd was in for one big surprise when instead of what was promised, a magnificent rendition of a 'Bellowing Stag', the flabbergasted mayor revealed a large piece of cloth depicting a crudely drawn forest with no stag in sight. Went for little stags, be back in five.

Upon closer examination, – since some of the attendees had begun speculating whether this was a piece of abstract contemporary art – it was discovered that the cloth bore the signature of the donator's very own son. Though Philip Shyttles, 15, was adamant in his insistence that he "didn't do it", Mister Shyttles informed everyone present that his son would be grounded until he finished high school. The editor of this newspaper, however, is inclined to believe young Mister Shyttles, since even the most half-brained of criminals wouldn't be stupid enough to sign the crime scene.

When Georgy laid down the Newspaper, he could feel a blush blooming on his face. Okay, so maybe signing the thing with Philip's name had been a bit much but it had seemed like a hilarious idea at the time. He quickly re-read the article and glanced at the picture of the bedsheet printed underneath it.

"Was that you?" That morning Anna came up to him with all the intent of a raging bull. She didn't even give him enough time to answer before she grabbed him by the shoulders and planted a noisy kiss on his cheek that made his teeth rattle. "I swear, that was the funniest thing I have ever seen in my entire life! You should have seen the faces! When they first discovered Philip's signature, most people thought it was funny and that dumbass got up and bowed! Can you believe it? Then his dad went nuts on him and he immediately switched to whining and insisting he hadn't done it."

Since Philip was at least partially at fault for his own misfortune, being a pompous jackass and all, Georgy didn't feel all that guilty over the comments and the laughter that followed the guy wherever he went that day. Still, he decided not to chime in with the others because not only was it low-hanging fruit but also because he was having a good time as a silent observer.

Things almost came to a head during recess. Georgy, Olly and Raff were standing together in their usual corner and Olly was showing them a mint copy of an old comic book he had gotten from his uncle. They heard Philip coming before they saw him, mostly excuse everyone and their mother didn't seem to be able resisting the urge to give some snide remark at his passing. "Hey Shyttles, not sure if painter is the career path for you." "How could you possibly be dumb enough to sign with your own name? Were you

149

dropped as a child or something." "I'm just surprised he knows how to spell his name." The three of them watched idly as he approached, one of his cronies on each side like unusually round-faced, undergrown bodyguards. He seemed to be in a terrible mood. Georgy wasn't surprised. It must have been a tough pill to swallow; having people shrink away in fear when you came by one day, and having them laugh at you the next. Even Philip must have realized that he could hardly beat up the entire school. That thought brought a grin to Georgy's face. "What're you looking at?" Kevin hissed in their general direction once they came within earshot. "Just moved by this touching display of solidarity, is all." Raff shot back, wiping an imaginary tear from his eye. "Yeah." Georgy agreed with a lazy smile. "Chin up, Shyttles. People may think your art's trash now but give it another twenty years..." "You just don't know when to shut up, do you?" Kevin said dangerously but Raff was on a roll. "I can't help it, it's like watching the Stooges scale mount Doom." "You little..." Kevin took a step toward Raff, who immediately raised his fists, the grin gone from his face in a heartbeat. Georgy hardly noticed, though. Philip hadn't said anything yet. Instead he had just been staring, wordlessly and entirely transfixed, directly at Georgy's face like he was studying him. Kevin glance over his shoulder at Philip, waiting for a signal or something of the like. Philip finally looked away. His eyes landed on Olly and his mouth drew into a lazy smile. "What you got there, point Dexter?" He said in

150

a strange voice, a voice that sounded almost amicable. Olly gave a faint squeaking noise and shoved the comic book behind his back. It was an old Defenders Comic from 1972. Philip leisurely strolled toward him. "Lemme see." He said. Olly, who had gone very pale, looked over at Raff with wide eyes. Raff glanced at George. All of Georgy's thoughts had come to a screeching halt. They had fought with Philip and his gang before, they had taken a beating before. Why did this feel different? Philip took the comic from Olly's stiff hands, flipped it open, looked through the pages and everyone watched him as though they were in a trance.

With all the force he could presumably muster, Philip brought the comic book down on Olly's head. Instead of tearing it in half, Olly's head snapped to the front and he stumbled to his knees with something between a scream and a groan. The spell was broken. Raff, who seemed to have forgotten all about Kevin, whirled around and launched himself at Philip. Philip was carried a step by the momentum but managed to stay on his feet and pushed Raff off him with enough force to almost make him trip over Olly who was still cowering by their feet. For a moment, it seemed like he had caught his footing when-- Wham! Kevin had tackled him to the ground. The noise Raff made on impact finally stirred Georgy from his stupor. He stumbled forward and grabbed Kevin with both hands, trying to pry him off of Raff, his head buzzing, his ears ringing with laughter, while Kevin raised his fist and-

"What the hell do you think you're doing!?" Georgy felt himself be pushed to the side. "Do you think this is a zoo? Am I teaching monkeys? It's scum like you that makes me fear for the future of this country! This isn't funny Shyttles, stop laughing!" He recognized the voice of Mister Rampart, who was dragging Kevin off of Raff. Raff slowly got into a sitting position, there was blood running down his chin. Their eyes met for a moment and Georgy immediately recognized the expression on his friend's face. They seemed to be thinking the same thing. That could have gone far worse. Georgy lifted his head and looked over his shoulder, where Mister Rampart was escorting Kevin into the building and he noticed something else. Wally, Lisa and Urs were standing not too far away and watching them. Urs' eyes landed on Raff's face, now that it wasn't buried under 150 pounds of Kevin, she slapped her hand in front of her mouth and made a beeline toward them. "Did he hit you in the head?" She called, even before she had even reached them. "How many fingers am I holding up?" She didn't give Raff a chance to answer, however, took a pack of tissue paper out of her pocket and began dabbing away at his mouth. Even though teeth were tinted an unpleasant shade of red, Raff's face split into a dreamy smile. Wally and Lisa who had reached them now, hauled Olly, who was sneakily rubbing at his eyes to his feet. "Good talk." Philip said, as he looked at them, Georgy, Raff and Urs on the floor and Wally, Lisa and Olly standing huddled together in the corner. "Think we're done here, though." With that he tore the back out of the comic book he was still holding in his hands and chucked the loose pages in Olly's general direction. "Oh, and just so you know, Woodstock, it's cute how you look out for Tombstone all the time, getting your dad or your teacher friends to save his dumb butt. It's *like watching the Stooges scale mount Doom.*" He paused. "But I'm not sure if your Hippie floosy would appreciate me fixing your face like Urs does. But I guess in that case everything would have been an improvement, huh Raff?" At those words, Urs rose to her feet, glowering. She was a delicate girl with a mop of brown curls so big that it made her look even smaller in comparison. "You're a disgusting piece of shit, you know that?" She growled. Philip snorted. "Oh, no. Now I'm scared." Urs' eyebrows shot up and her eyes flashed for a fraction of a second, then she was suddenly standing in front of Philip, grabbed him by the arms and slammed her knee right between his legs. Philip's eyes grew three sizes, his cheeks puffed up and his breath hitched. The other guy who'd been with him, jumped to his side and grabbed him by the shoulder. As they limped away, Philip apparently struggling to put one foot in front of the other, Urs stared at their backs, her hands firmly planted on her hips. "As you better well should be!" She called out after them. "You're going to get yours soon enough!" The words rang a little hollow because Raff was still sitting on the floor, bleeding and with Olly hugging the pages of the comic to his chest. He might have been crying, Georgy couldn't tell.

153

Kevin had been suspended for a week and Philip was being more of a pain than usual. The thing was that he wasn't just yelling insults or picking fights anymore and he hadn't even once tried to clog the toilets- instead, he seemed to go out of his way to mess with people. One day, he would steal some prized action figure and have it dangling from the flagpole, the next he would make some poor sixth grader in a nice shirt wear his lunch. On the flipside, the swelling on Raff's face had gone down after about three days and the purple was fading into yellow. Raff himself was switching constantly between trying to get Urs to baby him and doing his best to look tough in front of his friends, which could have been hilarious, if Georgy hadn't been in the most terrible of moods since the birth of humanity. He hated that he hadn't done better in the fight, hated feeling helpless – hated Philip. And he was going to make sure that that guy wasn't going to get away with what he'd done. As if he hadn't been angry enough, he was soon to get an even greater incentive.

"What's wrong?" Lisa asked Anna during recess that day. She and Wally were spending the breaks between lessons with them again now, ever since the fight a few days ago but Georgy pretended like he had barely noticed. "Nothing." Anna said and shrugged but it didn't sound convincing. "So you're wearing that long-suffering look for our benefit?" Wally asked. Anna's mouth silently opened

154

and closed a couple of times, then she smiled – but it was that strange smile again. "Oh, you know..." She said. "Philip just won't take the hint and leave me alone." She laughed woodenly. "He seems to think that he's some sort of gang boss all of a sudden, the way he acts." The corners of her mouth twitched downward and she looked at her feet. "I half expect him to threaten me with going swimming with the-"She sobbed.   Lisa took a step forward and pulled her into a hug. Georgy stared at Anna's shaking shoulders, a familiar ringing in his ears. "Why the hell doesn't that asshole target someone else?" He hissed. "You're obviously not interested in buying. How's he going to turn a profit like that?" Anna sniffled. "Unless he isn't doing it for the money." Wally said. "Then what?" Raff asked shrilly. "You think he's doing it for the sake of recreation?" Wally shrugged and looked around, then he said, in a low voice: "I think he knows about the bell thing." Georgy felt his insides freeze and he remembered something Philip had said not too long ago. *I hear there are other things Thomson does to bells.* "What if he pieced together the thing with the painting from that?" "You don't know that, let's not jump to conclusions here." "He would have ratted on George then, though wouldn't he?" "Philip's not nearly smart enough for that.

Right?" Pandemonium. Everybody was talking all at once.

"We're going to stop him." Georgy said grimly and everyone quieted down. "And how are you going to do that?" Wally asked with raised eyebrows. "Let's go inside. Then I'll tell you."

A few minutes later, they were gathered around a desk in the boys' homeroom and Georgy began to explain: "Didn't you guys ask yourselves where the painting went?" "Wherever you stashed it." Wally deadpanned. "I imagine it would still be there." "Yeah, didn't you say you hid it in the town hall?" Raff asked. Georgy nodded. "Behind a shelf. Pretty sure it would have made the news had they found it." "So... How's that help us?" Asked Anna. "You already framed Philip for stealing it." Georgy considered for a moment, then he nodded again. "True. So the next step would be... to get myself some weed." Nobody said anything for a moment. Wally's eyes narrowed at him, Urs, Anna and Raff exchanged quizzical looks and even Lisa quirked a brow. "You know." Wally said, very slowly. "If you're short of ideas, there are better ways to get creative." Raff nodded animatedly. "Like, pretty much anything else. And I'm sure we could figure something out if we put our heads together." He looked at the others. "Right, guys?" There was a murmur of agreement and now it was Georgy's turn to stare at them. He wasn't sure whether to be amused or offended. "Easy there." He said. "I don't need it for myself. You see, I thought we'd slip a note into Philip's pocket. Something along the lines of 'Hey, you want the painting, come to the specified location at the specified time and get it back'-sort of thing. All he would have to do is claim that he figured the painting was likely exchanged in town hall. Like: 'The thief probably knew that sneaking the thing out would have looked suspicious.'" There was a short-lived silence again. Judging by the look on Raff's face, he thought Georgy had gone off the deep end for good. "That's not all." Georgy continued but Raff cut him off. "No, don't tell me." He said. "Then you sign it with your own name this time." "No." Georgy snapped impatiently. "If you'd just let me finish. I'll hide the stuff there as well. Then we watch him - and when he goes to pick up the painting, we call the cops. Criminals return to the scene of the crime, you know. That's what they'll think. The painting is found, Philip get busted for possession. Everyone wins."

"I don't think you need to buy anything." Anna said quietly, twisting a string of black hair around a finger. "Lars may still have some stuff stashed away in his room and I think..." She paused for a moment, then she nodded to herself. "I think I may just know where." "Good thinking." Georgy said although the idea had already crossed his mind as well. Buying drugs wasn't exactly something he fancied adding to his repertoire. "You sure it's still there though?" "Probably. Not like he got any chances to, uh, light up lately, as it were. And I know for a fact that nobody touched that 1000-dollar hooch he had saved for himself for the longest time." Georgy raised a brow at her. "What do you mean for the 'longest time'?" Anna beamed at him. "The Waste collectors were very appreciative."

Anna delivered. During recess the next day, when Georgy had just sat down to watch Olly and Raff play a rather violent game of tether-ball, sandwich unwrapped and ready to go, she plopped down next to him. He could tell that something was up by the way she shifted uncomfortably in place and when she pulled a lumpy looking sock from under her jumper, he knew he had been right. Without a word, he took the sock from her hands and when he slipped it into the pocket of his cargos, sandwich now forgotten on the bench beside him, it hit him like a brick to the gut. If he got caught now, he'd be in for a world of trouble. Judging by the hand that was suddenly atop of his, Anna had sensed his thoughts. "It's weird." She said with a hoarse chuckle. "It kinda looks like dried up broccoli. Chunky, you know. No idea how you would go about smoking it." "You looked at it?" It was more of a statement than a question. Georgy felt weird. All he could think was that he didn't need a visual. That he didn't want one. The sock felt heavy in his pocket. Anna shrugged and tilted her head into the sun. Then she sighed. "Had to. Found more than we bargained for in Lars' room last night. Pills and powders. And gallons of booze, of course." "We?" Anna hesitated for a moment. "Yeah." She said and it sounded like a confession. "I didn't even know what I was looking for. Never even peeked at the stuff when I bought it. So I had to enlist Arty's help. Turns out he was big into the hippie movement once." Georgy said nothing so she continued. "But don't worry about it. He's pretty cool and he doesn't ask questions. He's like my own personal Alfred." When Georgy still didn't respond, she fell quiet for a while. He could feel her eyes on the side of his head like hot embers. This wasn't how it was supposed to be and for the hundredth time in the last week, he wondered how the hell he had allowed it to get that way. Probably realizing that the conversation wasn't likely to go anywhere anymore, Anna sighed again. "This is big, George." She said. "Real big. I mean..." She ran a hand through her hair. "Philip? He's just a little fish. Even if we get rid of him, even if the plan works out – the real problem..." "The Frenchman will still be out there." Georgy mumbled. "Exactly." She shifted on her spot next to him. Her voice was soft when she spoke again. "Listen: I know you think..." She shook her head. "Like, you have to, you know, do this. But no one would think less of you if you ducked out of the race if you think the stakes are too high. Least of all me." She gave him a warm smile, but he barely noticed. He could feel the sock press into his thigh through the fabric of his pants. It was like an anchor that chained him to something – something scary and foreboding that was dragging him in a strange direction toward an unknown destiny. Olly grunted, when the tetherball smacked him square in the face. "Sorry man." Raff said when he jogged over to survey the damage. "But you should have seen that coming."

Georgy stopped by the town hall on his way home. That time around, the building seemed entirely different, bustling with activity as it was. People were going in and out as they pleased and so it was no trouble at all to slip in as well without rousing suspicion. The closer he got to the conference room, the more excited he got. He looked around and for a brief moment, his eyes landed on the outer edges of something that was peeking out from behind a shelf ever   so   slightly.

He absentmindedly noted that someone must have forgotten to close the door. Could he risk taking a look? What would be the harm? He couldn't help but grin when he saw that they hadn't taken the bedsheet down. Perhaps he had more artistic talent than expected   after   all. "May I help you?" Georgy spun around and blushed furiously when he realized there was a man standing behind him. How had he not noticed before? When the man gave him a smile, he relaxed a little. "Wanted to see for yourself, eh? I swear, this place hasn't seen so many young people since they used it as a bomb shelter." The man laughed amicably. "Maybe we should have an exhibition on vandalism, huh? That would draw you in like moths to a flame." Georgy was feeling more and more uncomfortable with every word that came out of the man's mouth and so he just quickly excused himself and took off.

The next day the plan entered the first phase. Georgy had just told Raff that he was going to make sure to be the last to leave the classroom, when Urs unceremoniously plopped down in the latter's lap. "Right on cue." Georgy said, tapping the desk for emphasis. "She does have great timing." Raff mumbled dreamily. Urs craned her head back and gave him what must have been a very sloppy kiss. "Gross." Georgy muttered and made a show of turning away. "Avert your eyes all you like." Raff said between smooching noises and touching noses. "I already saw them flash green." " I think the green-eyed monster is for when you're jealous, not green with envy." Urs told him. Raff finally stopped kissing her at that. "What's the difference?" He asked, his brows furrowed. "Envy means you want something. Jealousy means you want someone." She giggled. "And that's not me now, is it?" Georgy felt his face heating up but Raff just shrugged. "From where I'm sitting, as it happens -" He waggled his eyebrows at her. "I'm the luckiest guy here one way or the other." "Anyway..." Georgy cut in because Urs looked about ready to suck Raff's face off at those words and he wasn't sure his stomach could handle that. "Philip. The note. Focus people." When the two of them turned to him with what could be described as mild curiosity at best, he lowered his voice and quickly continued. "Can you distract Mister Brightman for me, Urs? Just in case he thinks he's back in 'Nam again and decides, no man should be left behind in the classroom." Urs nodded. Raff saluted her. "Raff, you need to distract whoever has classroom duty today. Anyone know who that is?" "That would be Hailey." Said Wally, leaning in over Georgy's

161

shoulder. "Hey there." Urs grinned up at him. "You in on this, too?" "Wouldn't think it, scarce as he's making himself these days." Georgy grumbled sullenly and leaned a little to the side because Wally's sleeve was brushing his arm. "Didn't mean to hurt your feelings or nothin'." Wally said with a sardonic grin. "You know you are the only one for me." "I'll take care of Hailey." Raff said only to shrink away at the venomous glare Urs gave him. "Well, it wouldn't make a lick of sense for you to flirt with her." He mumbled defensively. "What, so you don't mind if I flirt with Mister Brightman?" "Don't be ridiculous. Can't you just take one for the-" "I'll slip the not into Philip's bag once nobody's looking." Georgy cut them off again; this time because he had the sneaking suspicion that Raff wouldn't live to see the end of recess if he finished that sentence. "That way, he'll find it when he gets home." "I like it." Raff nodded, stubbornly avoiding any eye contact with Urs who was still glowering at him. "Short and easy to remember." "Kind of overly reliant on the assumption that Philip so much as touches his schoolbag when he gets home though." Wally said. "Well, I did considered stapling it to his forehead but I just couldn't figure out how to make that work." Georgy snapped. "And anyway. That's why we'll keep an eye on him. He'll want to restore his good name once he figures it out." "His good name?" Raff snorted. "What's a good name by Shyttles-standards?" "One without a warrant attached to it."

162

Urs spent math class writing up a Philip-Surveillance schedule for the coming week. It required teams of two people to follow him from the last bell at 3 pm to around 5 pm when town hall was locked up for the day. Georgy noticed that she apparently had made sure that Raff wasn't paired up with any girls other than Urs herself, but he pretended that he hadn't.

Everything worked out a little too well after that, and in hindsight Georgy felt like he should have known. Slipping the note into Philip's bag had been child's play – all that was left after that was to wait, all the while making sure everyone knew whom to call once stuff hit the fan. Namely the police.

They discussed their plan with Olly, Anna and Lisa during recess and although Anna pouted a bit when she realized that she wasn't scheduled to get in on the action till the middle of the week, nobody had had any major complaints. "I really hope this works." The bell rang just when Georgy had finished drawing a very crude map of the area surrounding the town hall to demonstrate where exactly the payphone could be found and students began filling back into the building. "Hey." Wally had stopped moving and was looking at him expectantly. Georgy glanced over his shoulder. The others had already vanished into the crowd trying to squeeze through the door all at once. "You think people are gonna believe it? That Philip would be dumb enough to try and smuggle the painting out of town hall?" Georgy shrugged. "Maybe not within context. The individual parts of the story though?" He nodded. "Philip will be there when we call the police, so will the painting and the other stuff." Wally stood there, with a far-away expression on his face. "It's real messed up." He said. "Like when they just believed he had stolen the thing in the first place without any proof. Real messed up." Georgy shrugged again. What did Wally care if Philip got into trouble? It wasn't like he didn't have it coming. "It's his own fault." He muttered. "He basically confessed right there and then. And what's it matter to you, anyway? That guy's a menace." Wally snorted, usual grin locked in place again. "Totally missing the point there. But anyway." He pointed at the door. "Let's get going before the ground gives way beneath our feet, yeah?"

It took until Thursday, then his phone rang. He looked at his watch: A quarter to four. He jumped off the couch, raced into the hallway and plucked the handset off the switch so fast that it almost flew right out of his hand. "Yeah?" "George, is that you?" It was Anna and judging by the way her voice sounded, she was having the time of her life. "Yeah, it's me. Did something happen?" "You won't believe it!" She squeed. "They got him!" There was a brief pause during which Georgy let that sink in. "Did they find the, uh, package?" He asked. "I think so. I told them that Philip was holding when I called, at any rate. But man, did we ever high-tail it out of there. I'm not sure when the police questions people or how they pick 'em but Olly's twitchy enough when things are calm, so..." "Yeah, yeah. Good call. As long as nobody saw you."

"Sure thing. But will I be seeing *you* again today?", Anna's voice sounded unusually cautious and a little too casual. "Uh, sure if you... You know, wouldn't rather..." Rest? Do anything other than hang out with me one on one? Georgy didn't get the chance to think of a proper end to that sentence because Anna cut him off. "George." She said in a deadpan voice. "I asked." "Oh." That moment he vividly remembered what Wally had said to Raff not too long ago. *If you just talked to her like a human being.* "Uh, sure. I'd like that." His voice sounded strange to his own ears. "Would you? Terrific." Anna said with a sigh and Georgy could practically hear her roll her eyes. "Do you want me to talk to your dad now? You know, so I can return you before curfew." "Hey, that was uncalled for." He muttered and Anna giggled. "In an hour at the old playground." She said. "Don't be late or I'll make you pay for your own dinner." Georgy could feel his heart do as summersault in his chest and a chuckle bubbling up in his throat. "Good plan. Have you ever dined and dashed before?" "No I haven't. Sounds exciting. Maybe we should try sometime." It was funny, how she could be so enthusiastic about something like that but Georgy wouldn't have dreamed of actually going through with it. "Changed my mind. We're not doing that. And if I have to go slave away in a factory or something so I can take you out properly." "That..." Anna began, voice suddenly lacking any venom and Georgy realized what he had just said, face hot as a stove within seconds. "That's really sweet." "You just might have to wait until summer." He mumbled. "We could, I don't know, maybe go for ice cream..." "*I* would like that." She said. "See you in an hour?"

A thousand thoughts of unfamiliar things were rushing through his head all at once. Things he'd read about, things he'd seen in movies. Holding Anna, kissing her. The way her cheeks dimpled when she smiled, the sound of her laughter and all the times she had leaned in close to kiss his cheek. How easy it would have been to just turn his head to the side and have their lips touch instead. He shook his head, swerving dangerously to the side and had to stop his bike for a moment. Now was not the time to overthink things, he told himself. Now was the time to act. When he reached the playground, Anna was already sitting on a swing, swaying gently back and forth without her feet leaving the ground.

"Uh, hi." Georgy looked at her expectantly but when she didn't even raise her head, he wordlessly lowered himself onto the second swing. "Hi." She said quietly. "The plan was great. I can't believe it went off without a hitch." Why did you doubt it when you thought it was great, Georgy almost asked but he caught himself? Instead, they sat in silence for a while. Yet again, he remembered Wally's words with amazing clarity. Like a human being. Like a human being. *Like a human being.* He gave her a quick sidelong glance. She had tipped her head to the side, ear resting against the rope and was unabashedly grinning at him. She was messing with him. Somehow, that realization just spurred him on. "Anna?" - "Yeeees?" - "Anna, there's something I've been meaning to ask." Her head shot around so she was staring him dead in the eye and he was caught so off guard that he faltered a little. It felt like somebody had stuck his head someplace where there was too little air. "Meaning to ask?" She echoed in a singsong voice. He knew that he could have made it all a big joke, right then, that he could have made it easy, just leaned over and kissed her and have her crack wise after – but he was going to do it his way. "I like you." He said simply. "I like you a lot." The smile didn't fade from Anna's face, instead it turned impossibly more beautiful. "I thought you'd never ask." She sighed, pushed her swing closer to his with one foot and kissed him. On his way home, it felt like he was actually flying. Things couldn't have been better, he felt. Forgotten were all the troubles of the preceding weeks. It didn't last long, however. When he rolled onto the driveway, he noticed someone standing in front of the building. Upon closer inspection, it turned out to be Mister Woodman.

He didn't look happy.

Chapter 8   Jumping Geraniums

When they had first met in their third year of elementary school both of them little leaguers, Wally had been a twitchy kid. Georgy vividly remembered a time, when some other boy had accidentally bloodied Wally's nose with a bat and when Mister Woodman had come to pick him after practice, instead of comforting his son or at least asking what had happened, he had smacked him upside the head. Georgy had told his mother about it later and after considering for a moment, she had sighed and said that sometimes people weren't great at expressing their concern with words, so they did it differently. Needless to say that Georgy had not at all been convinced.   The intensity with which Mister Woodman had glowered at his son had been as far away from concern as he had been from being able to buy one of those remote-controlled racing cars he'd seen   on   TV. And it was that same intensity that he was being stared   at   with   right   then. "All I want to know." Mister Woodman said through gritted teeth. "Is who did this to my son." Georgy glanced at his dad. He'd never seen him looking so grave. "It wasn't George, Wallace." He said. "They are friends. Maybe your son had trouble with other kids-" "Pah!" Mister Woodman scoffed. "I didn't raise no wuss." And to Georgy's surprise, there was something like pride swinging in his voice. "If my boy ain't talkin' it's because he's protecting someone." He glared at Georgy again who suddenly felt a strange lump in his throat. "You friends with my son, boy?" He asked. "Yes, Sir." Georgy croaked. "I am." "Then where were you when he got his nose bridge smashed into his forehead?" Georgy vaguely registered his dad mumbling something in Spanish. It felt like the ground had cracked open beneath his feet. "I was..." He began. "I was... meeting someone. A girl." "That what you kids do, that all you think about. Hanging around some girl when you're fourteen, know jack about the world-" "Wallace." Georgy's dad interrupted him, exasperation in his voice. As if to make some silent point, he took a step toward the other man, his arms extended on both sides but Mister Woodman didn't back down. "You know what he say to me? You know what he say to me, Juan?" Georgy's dad didn't say anything. "He say it's a gift." Mister Woodman's nostrils flared. "He say it's a farewell-gift from that friend of his that gone leave the country." "George isn't going anywhere, Wallace." Georgy's dad said, his voice sounding very strained. "Which friend?" Georgy asked. Mister Woodman huffed. "The one that got a scholarship or something'. For some wack painting he did. And you're an artsy kid, so-" Georgy wasn't listening anymore. His mind was reeling. Without a second thought, he jumped back onto his bike and started paddling. Mister Woodman was screaming something, his dad was screaming something but he almost didn't   hear   it.

169

"Good news. Philip's leaving the country. Got it right from the horse's mouth." Even though there were bandages running around his head, Georgy could tell that Wally was smirking, sitting on his bed, a box of tissues on his lap, more tissues stained with blood on the floor around him. It seemed his bandages were leaking and the skin around his eyes looked purple and swollen. Georgy couldn't think of anything to say. Instead, he pulled up the chair from Wally's desk and slid onto it. He stared at his knees; Wally tapped a rhythm on the cardboard box, then chuckled. "You look like somebody died." He said and something in his voice made Georgy's face flush with shame. "It's just a broken nose. Or are you mad that you weren't the one who got it?" "No!" Georgy hissed and glared at him. Wally shrugged. "Just saying. Anna's into scars, right?" They fell silent again, Georgy scrambling for something to say. He noticed that his hands were choking the air in front of him and he smoothed them against his thighs. "Look." He began. "If you… If you're… If you want…" Wally cut him off. "You waiting for an 'I-told-you-so'? I'm not the type. If you're fixing to apologize to someone though, I'd try Olly. He got his lip busted trying to help me." Georgy's mouth twitched but before he could get any words out, the door to Wally's room swung open, revealing Mister Woodman. The two of them stared at each other for a moment then Mister Woodman's mouth pulled into a sneer. "Your little friend here?" "Yeah, dad." Wally replied. "But he was just leaving." Georgy's head snapped around to look at Wally, who was smirking as always. Mister Woodman nodded and closed the door without another word. Georgy gave Wally a questioning look and Wally raised his eyebrows as if he were waiting for something. Georgy awkwardly got up from the chair and slowly walked to the door. He looked over his shoulder but Wally sat on his bed like he had turned to stone. "You should be happier." He said. "Your plan worked out in the end." Georgy shook his head. He knew that he had to say something. "Listen man, I-!" But again, Wally cut him off. "Forget it, George. Just forget it."

The next morning his mood seemed to change by the minute while, he rode to school. He was confused when he thought about Anna, he was happy. Then his thoughts would shift to Philip and his gang and he'd be enraged, then he'd be proud, then he'd think of Wally and his chest ached. At least Philip wasn't there and, sure enough, by second period the entire school knew that Philip Shyttles had been expelled for good. When Miss Sanders informed the class that he wasn't going to return, even though they had known already, Raff gave Georgy a thumbs up. More than anything, however, Georgy wanted it to be recess. When the bell rang he raced down into the courtyard.

Waiting in front of the exit that Anna used nine times out of ten, he could barely contain his excitement. When she rounded the corner, however, his face fell. Kevin was walking next to her and by the looks of it he was having an animated conversation – one that didn't require her participation whatsoever. Just like that (and as per usual as of late) Georgy's mood shifted. This time, however, he knew that he could do what needed to be done. Purposefully, he strode toward the pair and fueled by a sudden surge of furious confidence; he grabbed Kevin by the sleeve and yanked him to the side without a moment's hesitation. It felt good. Before Kevin got out so much as a peep, Georgy was stabbing his finger into his chest. "You listen here." He hissed. "You leave her the hell alone or I'll make sure that you get the same as Philip." With a quick movement of his arm, Kevin shook off Georgy's hand and gave him a look that was equal parts defiance and suspicion. "What crawled up your butt, Tombstone? A maggot?" He chuckled at his own joke but his eyes darted about nervously. "Your parents rich too, Kev?" Georgy said quietly, so that only Kevin could hear. "They got enough money to whisk you away to a private school in Switzerland or Britain if you mess up? Make you go away for a while till things blow over?" Kevin stared at him, wide-eyed. "What do you mean?" He whispered his voice suddenly hoarse. "I mean." Georgy said very slowly. "You." And he punctuated the word with a jab of his finger. "Leave. Her. The hell. Alone." Anna, who hadn't said anything the entire time, was watching them in enraptured silence. "Did he try to get you to buy something?" Georgy indicated Kevin with a jerk of his head. "Yeah, he did." She said matter-of-factly. "It seems he fancies himself the new big-boss

172

around here." She gave Kevin a disgusted glare that made Georgy's knees weak even though it wasn't directed at him. Silently, he vowed to never give her a reason to look at him that way. "I'll cut you a deal, Kev." He said, trying for friendly and landing on strained. "You stop bothering Anna and you stay out of juvie. Sound good?" When Kevin's brows shot up like the cork out off a bottle, Georgy realized that maybe that had been laying it on thick. "Daydreaming again, Tombstone?" He asked snidely. "You ain't got that kind of pull with anyone." "What happened to Philip?" Anna countered. "Do you know? You're pals, right?" "Non-a-ya beeswax." Kevin said, reclining a bit where he stood and fishing a pack of cigarettes out of his pocket. "But the Switzerland-thing wasn't that far off." He fingered a cigarette out of the box and lit it. "Not that bad a deal, if you ask me." He said. "Real distinguished-like over there. Real classy. Although..." He took a drag. "This ain't so bad either." "Gunning a stick by the dumpster sure is living large." Anna muttered. "Square." Kevin mumbled. "Whatever." Georgy grunted. This entire conversation wasn't going anywhere. "You bug Anna, I make you sorry. Got it?" "You bug me I break somebody's nose." Kevin shot back. Then he blew a plume of smoke in Georgy's face. Georgy turned his head away on instinct, sputtering. "Suck it." Kevin said, turned on his heels and stalked off.

Anna put her arm around George and gave him a smile. "Think he got it?" He asked. "Maybe." She said and gave him a kiss. "But even if he leaves me alone, he'll still be trying to peddle that stuff to other kids." Georgy took a deep breath. "There's no getting around that. Unless we actually, you know... put him out of business, too."

When they joined the others standing in their usual spot in the courtyard, Georgy was far too distracted by trying to figure out a way to get rid of Kevin to pay attention to the conversation. He was stirred from his thoughts, however, when he heard his own name. "Since Anna and Georgy are a thing now." Urs had just finished with a flourish of her hand, followed by wide-eyed silence on the parts of Olly and Raff. "You're a thing now?" Raff asked, turning to George who was trying to avoid eye contact with Olly who looked at him as though Urs had just announced he had flown up to the moon on a paper-glider. "What a surprise." Wally muttered with a role of his eyes. "Why didn't you tell us?" Raff demanded but didn't give him a chance to answer. "All these years I've groomed you, taught you everything I know and then-" "We wanted to announce it when we had all of you in one place." Anna said with a shrug. "That's why you told Urs, huh?" Raff said, pointing an accusing finger at her. "I knew, too." Lisa cut in, raising her hand. "Me, too." Wally said. Raff threw up his hands theatrically. "You told everyone except me." "Not really." Wally shrugged. "I figured it out by myself. It was kind of obvious." "I didn't know either." Said Olly. With a very fake sounding snivel

Raff pulled Olly against his side. "Let's go." He said. "We're obviously not wanted here." "Oh, c'mon." Anna said with a snort. "It's not like you'll never see him again." And with a grin in Georgy's direction, she added: "Just give me a call if you want to schedule a playdate." "We'll just take him on the weekends, once you get tired of him." Wally said with a shrug. Somehow, that comment stung. "Awesome." Urs said. "Now that that's settled, what about that triple date at the movies?" "That's not coming out of our time." Raff said indignantly and Georgy knew that if he didn't cut them off now, his friends would keep themselves going until recess was over.

"Before we get to the fun part." He said. "It seems that now that Philip's gone, Kevin's taken his place." Urs shook her head with an exasperated sigh. "That gang of theirs is like a chimera." She said. "What's a chimera?" Asked Olly. "I take it you have a plan?" Asked Wally. "Not yet." Georgy said. "But he's chicken, I think. He doesn't have a rich dad backing him up, like Philip did." "So maybe we can scare him into backing off?" Anna asked. "And how'd we do that?" Georgy thought about that for a moment.

"Maybe we can follow him the next time he goes to hang at that shed of his dad's?" Raff nodded. "Just need to find a way to get in there somehow." "Wh-why would you want to get in?" Olly asked a waver in his voice. Georgy gave him a quick once over. The way Olly looked, hunched over and sort of afraid, he just couldn't imagine him jumping into the fray to help anyone. "To figure out what he stashes in that place." Raff said, shrugging nonchalantly. "And it would be the perfect opportunity, to send him a... warning, shall we say?" "Sounds good." Anna agreed. "I vote blood on the walls." "Not bad." Georgy said with a grin. "Though I'm drawing a blank on the execution, other than raiding a blood bank, I mean. So I guess a letter will have to do." There was a murmur of agreement and Georgy considered for a moment. "Make it real official-like." He said. "Fed-official?" Raff asked, grinning with anticipation. "Something like that. We'll write that we confiscated the, uh, contraband that Kevin will undoubtedly have hidden in the shed and that, if the need arises, we would take action. If he doesn't lay low for a while, he'll get the same as Philip." "Could work." Anna mumbled, slowly nodding to herself. "Except... You kind of already told him that it was you who got rid of Philip." Georgy shrugged. "Maybe he'll think I was bluffing. Maybe he'll even manage to put two and two together once in his life. Good for him. The point is, he gets that there's somebody who doesn't kid around." He gave the others a meaningful look, to mixed results. Olly for one looked so utterly not on board, that Georgy quickly decided that ominous maybe didn't work for him. "I'll write the letter." Lisa offered, seeming as oblivious as ever. "I thought Anna could..." Georgy started but Anna resolutely cut him off. "Lisa's dad is a lawyer." She said with a tight-lipped smile. "If you

176

want it to sound 'official-like' she's the way to go." Georgy stared at Anna, who shrugged defensively and avoided his eyes. Raff gave the two of them a weird look. "What was that about?" He asked. Silently, Georgy cursed Raff's lack of timing and general sense of tact. He didn't get around to answering, however, because Wally had already clasped a hand over Raff's shoulder and said with a grin that was half lost under his bandages: "Probably save the writing for their secret correspondences or something." A strong feeling of gratitude bloomed in the pit of Georgy's stomach. Whatever warped, messed up thing had been going on between Wally and him as of late, that moment it felt like it all hadn't been real. He mumbled a thanks. Wally gave him a wink.

Raff and Wally were the lookouts while Georgy worked open the lock with a bent piece of wire. The door opened with a low growl and Anna, Olly, Lisa and George slipped into the shed. Ten minutes later, Anna found what they had been looking for in a cardboard box between the compost and the fertilizer. It was wrapped in the kind of brown paper that she had seen so many times before that she didn't even need to look inside. Based on her description what to make the decoy out of had been a tie between oregano and freeze-dried broccoli. After discovering that none of his friends just happened to have a freeze-drier sitting around at home, he settled on the former. While he carefully poured the oregano onto the paper, they couldn't help but giggle. "Just imagine the look on Kevin's face when he gets a whiff of this." Georgy mumbled. "Don't think anybody will be able to tell the difference." She whispered. "Oh, I don't know about that." Lisa chimed in, smiling serenely. "I'm certain it will be an improvement."

It took Kevin about three days to figure it out. The second he did, however, he didn't even try to hide it. One morning he barged into the classroom, fists clenched by his sides and head a vibrant shade of crimson. For a brief moment, he scanned the room, huffing and puffing like a raging bull, then his eyes zeroed in on George, who raised his hands and gave Kevin his best innocent look. "You!" Kevin growled. "You dirty, little-!" At the unmitigated rage in Kevin's eyes, Georgy couldn't help but take a step back and raise his hands little higher. He hadn't expected a reaction like that. Raff and Wally had gotten up from their respective seats and were now standing next to him. Kevin, whose mouth had been moving without a sound, sharply turned his head, his beady eyes landing on Wally. The bandages were gone but his face was covered in vibrant green and purple bruises and there was an obvious crank in his nose that hadn't been there before. Kevin's breathing slowed down. "What's your problem?" Wally asked nonchalantly. Kevin nodded as he turned back to George. "Don't you get..." He mumbled. "What happens when you don't leave well enough alone?" His nostrils flared dangerously. "People get

178

hurt when they stick their noses where they don't belong." His gaze wandered from one face to the next, eyes suddenly unfocused as though he didn't see them at all. Then he nodded again, turned on his heels and wandered off.

Things didn't stay calm for long. When they were standing in their usual spot during recess, Olly brought bad news. "Do you think Kevin had a second stash in the shed?" He asked in a hushed voice, nervously glancing over his shoulder. Georgy's eyebrows shot up into his hairline and Raff half choked on his ham sandwich. Wally motioned for Olly to go on. "It's just..." He stuttered. "I just saw him make a sale. Brown paper and everything." Anna cursed under her breath. "Guess that guy is smarter than we gave him credit for." She muttered. "Hold on." Raff said, placatingly raising his hands. "How do we know that he didn't just get new supplies from the Frenchman?" "Because Kev's still got all his ribs where they belong." Urs responded. "Regardless." Georgy rejoined. "Seems like Kevin didn't get the message." He gave a grim nod. "Which means that our work is not done yet."

So Urs created the Kevin-surveillance-schedule 2.0, which was immediately less popular than the first one because it required daily rotations.

Time seemed to stretch out infinitely when they shadowed Kevin now, like the worst kind of old gum. It took until Sunday for anyone to turn up something

179

new – And it wasn't what they had hoped for. "He's hiding it at home." Wally announced. "On his balcony. Buried it in a flower pot." There was a momentary silence. Georgy thoughtfully tapped his chin "Yeah, I saw him fussing over those dumb things, too. Just like my mom does. Waters them, prunes them – the whole shebang." Raff looked from Wally to George like he was trying to figure out if they were serious. "Slow down." He said. "I mean, I saw him fawning over those flowers, too. But who's to say that he isn't just really into gardening?" "Well, it is suspicious." Anna said as if she had just remembered something. "On two occasions I'm pretty sure it *was* the first thing he did after coming back from school." "And getting out of bed on the weekends." Olly added excitedly. "It is lead, at any rate." Georgy said with a broad grin. "Good work, man." Wally shook his head, indicating Lisa with his hand. All eyes turned to her where she stood, smiling serenely. "I saw him pour rice in there." She said. "Alright." Georgy said happily. Raff sighed. "Let's skip the part where I suggest that you're nuttier than a squirrel in fall and get straight to you explaining what you mean by that." Georgy gave a shrug. "Well, we know where he hides his stuff, for one. And he does it at fixed times." "Get to the point." Urs said rolling her eyes. Georgy couldn't help but pout a little but he went on anyway. "Remember that experiment with the sodium and the water in the Chemlab?" "Of course." Raff said. "Explosions are the best part of that course." "And the only part you're awake for." Wally shrugged. "So if we put some of that stuff in the flowerpots and he waters them..." "They'll blow up in his face." Anna exclaimed, theatrically raising her hands. "You're an evil genius!" "Where'll you get the sodium, genius?" Wally asked dryly. "There, is some at school..." Georgy began carefully and Wally rolled his eyes. "Whatever." He said. "Come get the key at my place." And running his hands though his hair, he added: "I can't wait for this entire thing to be over."

Georgy had remembered that raw Sodium was usually stored in some kind of oil-like paraffin. After scrounging around the basement for a while, he turned up an old lamp they used for camping and had poured some of its contents into a small bottle. That had been step one of his plan, step two was getting into school, which he could probably have done in his sleep by now. Raiding the Chemlab was a matter of minutes.

The next day, around three in the afternoon, he was sitting on the balcony at home, one of his mother's flowerpots on the ground before him. He took a small piece of sodium out of the bottle with some tweezers and slipped it down the side of the pot, where he'd dug a narrow trench. Then he poured on some water. It took about twenty seconds, then a plume of white smoke rose from the soil, like one of those Clun soda volcanos that tended to flood the local science fair.

It took a few more tries for him to figure out how to make the flowers move in the pot, though. The only thing that he knew could potentially make things difficult along the way, was that the reaction needed a certain amount of water to reach the sodium to trigger. His solution was a piece of wire mesh that he had positioned on two halved corks above the powder. On top of the mesh, he put a piece of cling wrap the same size as the flowerpot. In the center of the wrap, he had cut a sizable hole. The idea was bending the mesh in such a way that it would work like a funnel, that would direct the water directly onto the small chunk of sodium at the bottom. He shoveled the soil back onto his construct and did his best to arrange the flowers so that they would look natural. Sure, they were sticking out a bit more than usual but it wasn't all that noticeable. Maybe Kevin would just believe that his babies had just gone through a spontaneous growth spurt.

Once he was satisfied with his handiwork, he called up Olly and Raff for a little demonstration and although the two of them knew what was about to happen the result still took them by surprise. "Cheese-and-crackers." Raff whistled. "If this doesn't drive home our point, I'm sure it'll at least give Kev a heart attack." Olly who was giving the flowerpot nervous looks from time to time, nodded his agreement. "If this doesn't scare him, we may as well give up." "Oh, you know." Georgy said, very pleased with himself. "I'm sure the letter that his parents are going to receive, will have an effect as well."

This time it was Anna who had written the letter, if only after George had hounded her for the better parts of Thursday and Friday. "I thought you liked writing." He had said, wringing his hands in exasperation. "And it's not like this has to be print-ready for – for some fancy newspaper or something." Thin-lipped and without a word, she had agreed in the end. Friday afternoon, the gang got back together to go over the plan one final time. It was decided that only two people would go – one to keep watch and one to plant the bomb. To Georgy's surprise, Wally volunteered. The two of them decided to meet at the convenience store close to where Kevin lived around two in the morning.

They deposited their bikes behind the store and walked down the street towards Kevin's house. There was a streetlamp close by which's dim light made their shadows look like tall black ghosts crawling across the walls. Kevin's house was surrounded by a white picket fence that they vaulted over without any difficulty. The ground floor balcony wasn't high off the ground, which made it easy to climb. Once Georgy had swung himself across the railing, he was relieved to see that Kevin had let the blinds down. He gave Wally a quick thumbs up, then he got to work. Giving himself a nod of encouragement, he slid over to the flowerpots, fingers skimming the tops of the leaves as he tried to guess which one hid Kevin's stash. Not that it mattered but he would have liked to maybe fill some soil into the container or maybe flood the thing. Just

183

out of spite, in case the explosions didn't ruin the stuff anyway. He picked the pot to the far right and lifted the Geraniums and all their roots out of the soil with one practiced movement. Carefully, he scraped some dirt off the roots so that they would fit into the pot better once he was done, then he got the sodium and his contraption into place. He put the flowers back where they belonged, then he repeated the procedure on the next pot and the one after that until he was done. With a deep sigh and his heart racing in his chest, he wiped some sweat off his forehead and got out a dustpan and a brush. This place wasn't like the school. Not only was he sitting there out in the open and in plain view for everyone to see but he also didn't know the neighborhood and couldn't at all gauge how dangerous it was. In the meantime, Wally had gone to drop the letter into the mailbox. Peering over the railing again, while he was sliding around on his knees in an effort to brush the dirt off the wood, he saw him around the corner and his chest felt a little lighter. Once he was done, the two of them snuck back to their bikes and hurried home.

It had been decided that the friends were going to meet behind the same convenience store around nine the next morning just so that they'd be able to enjoy the fruits of their labor from up close. Raff had even brought a bag of popcorn but Georgy was too on edge to eat any. They didn't have to wait long, maybe ten minutes, then somebody pulled up the blinds and

184

Kevin stepped onto the balcony. Curtains up, Georgy thought, chewing on his thumb. "What's he doing?" Olly whispered excitedly. The friends had hidden themselves behind a group of cars parked on the opposite side of the street and were peering at the balcony through the windows. Georgy silently prayed that Kevin wouldn't decide to check on his stash for some reason.

"Picked up the watering can." Raff whispered. He sounded tense. Anna had brought her camera again and took the first picture, quietly giggling to herself. Urs kicked her in the shin and she quieted down. Kevin, oblivious as could be, began watering his geraniums. "That's it." Georgy whispered to himself. "Keep it coming? Poor things are bone dry." As if Kevin had heard him, he emptied half the can, whistling to himself without a care in the world. "Any minute now." He mumbled.

And he was right. Fine, white smoke was rising noiselessly from the pot just as Kevin was about to set down the watering can. When it hit the ground with a loud clatter, drenching Kevin's pants, Georgy knew that the guy had finally noticed. With a guttural sound of fear, Kevin leapt backwards, colliding heavily with the screen door, which briefly rattled about in its frame, then folded under Kevin's weight and fell backward. Kevin gave a high-pitched scream, arms reaching wildly, as he stumbled out of sight. There was a low thud and the sound of something breaking, like he had knocked over a vase or something, followed by a sharp, resounding bang as the first set of geraniums flew into the air, raining wet clumps of dirt and pot fragments on Kevin's feet which were still sticking out across the threshold. When the second set of geraniums joined the first with even more impressive acrobatics, Kevin's feet only twitched a little, then he lay completely still.

There was a brief moment of utter silence.

Then the fire alarm went off.

The friends were staring over at the balcony, open-mouthed and in various states of awe and shock until Kevin stirred weakly. "Let's get out of here." Georgy hissed. "Before he snaps out of it." "Criminy." Raff called out over the wind as they were raising home. "For a moment there, I thought we'd killed him." "Taken years off his life, more like." Wally called back; the he glanced over to Anna. "Did you get some picture of the flowers in mid-air." "I tried." She said. "Difficult to time it just right. But I think I got one of his face." "I'll take a copy." Georgy grinned, then his face fell. "Just kind of sucks that the pots didn't make it. I should have considered that they may be to brittle to take the combustion." "What do you care?" Wally asked, irony swinging in his voice. "It's not like he didn't deserve it." Georgy didn't know what to say, especially when he realized that he had said something very similar to Wally not too long ago. ”Yes.“ Lisa said quietly. ”Too bad about the flowers.“

They would have died eventually anyway, Georgy realized a few days later. His mother's flowers, the ones he had used to practice, had wilted. From the outside, they had looked fine but when he dug up the roots, he realized that he had burned them to a crisp without   ever   noticing.

Chapter 9   The Frenchman

On Monday morning Raff, George and Urs were waiting for Kevin with bated breath. When he finally arrived, it was plain to see that his mood was at an all-time low. His eyes nervously flitted across the room, settling on his desk as though he expected it to blow up as well before he shuffled over. It was then or never. Georgy subtly gestured for the others to follow him. Time to see whether Kev had finally gotten the hint. "Hey." Urs began curtly. "You have a nice weekend, Kev?" "How's the garden?" Raff asked. Kevin was grimly looking from one face to the next, but he didn't say anything. "So." Georgy's voice sounded controlled. "I hope you finally got it. If not, let me make myself clear: If you don't stop expect to be contacted by the principal and the police sometime in the near future, same as Philip. As you may have noticed, we know what you're doing, so I'd suggest you stop." Kevin was glowering at Georgy, still without a word. If looks could kill, Georgy thought – but too bad for Kevin that they couldn't. He leaned forward so that his nose was almost touching Kevin's ear. Kevin didn't so much as flinch. "Who's the Frenchman." Georgy whispered. In a flash Kevin went ramrod-straight just as if Georgy had given him an electrical shock. "Not a chance." He hissed. "That guy's gonna kill me if I blab." Just then, the teacher entered the classroom. "Think about it." Georgy mumbled, turning his back but Kevin grabbed him by the arm and pulled him back. "No dice, Tombstone." He muttered. "Threaten me with suspension all you want. Sure beats eating out of a straw though." A few intense moments, they stared each other down, then Kevin let go of Georgy's arm.

And Kevin stuck to his guns. They could give him meaningful glances and gesture menacingly all they wanted, he wouldn't talk. The deciding moment came entirely unexpected. The friends were standing in their usual spot during recess, except for Wally and Lisa who were presumably hanging with Lisa's hippie friends again. Georgy was watching Raff drool over Urs reciting some lines for the next school play while Olly and Anna were exchanging comic books. A girl in a red shirt and glasses walked up to them. "Hey Anna, we're going over to Frenchie's. D'you want anything?" Anna shook her head without looking up from an issue of The Secret Society of Super Villains. "Nah thanks, not today." She said. It felt a little like Georgy's brain had just done a backflip and he couldn't help slapping a hand in front of his eyes. How had he not thought of it before. Anna gave him a concerned look. "You all right?" "What did your friend just say?" Looking even more concerned now, Anna looked at her friend walking some ways in the distance and back at George. "That she's going to Frenchie's'?" "Frenchie's!" Georgy exclaimed excitedly. It belongs to the principal's brother!" "Uhu." Anna mumbled. "So..." She cleared her throat. "You're saying...?" "The Frenchman! The guy selling stuff to

189

the students is a French guy. The principal is from France and he has a brother. And we know that the Frenchman somehow got access to the school." "All right, I'm following you." Said Raff, not sounding convinced. "But why would that guy need to break into school if he has a perfectly good restaurant one street over where he can do all his dealing without running the risk of being caught by Wally's dad?" Georgy deflated a little. Good point. "The pipe!" Anna hissed. "What?" George looked over at Olly in confusion. "Ohhh…" Raff whispered. "Frenchie's' had a burst pipe earlier this year." "Exactly." Anna said, a wide grin spreading across her face. "Don't you remember when I told you that we couldn't go there for lunch?" "You did?" "Yeah." Raff interjected. "Don't you remember that time she curved me into the next century?" "So we need to go to Frenchie's and see if it is the right guy." Said Olly. "You saw him, didn't you George?" Georgy thought about that for a moment. He'd seen someone at school, that one night when Philip had gotten the beating of his life – but he'd been scared out of his mind and only seen the guy from behind, to boot. "He… had long, slicked back hair that he wore in a ponytail." He said slowly, racking his brain for details. "What, that's it?" Raff asked, sounding distinctly disappointed. "What if he got his haircut since January?" "Well, I don't know if it is the right guy but the principal's brother does have long hair." Said Anna, her eyes gleaming. "What d'you think?" She said, turning to George. "Fancy some hot

190

coffee and a croissant? My treat." Georgy didn't say anything for a moment. He felt a bit of that all too familiar shame when he thought about Anna buying him food. She seemed to be able to sense his thoughts, however and made a hand gesture as if to bat them away. "If it bothers you so much, you can pay me back once you get your own money." "Without interest, I hope." He mumbled sheepishly. "Depends on the market." She said, grinning.

They had agreed to meet at Frenchie's at around three o'clock in the afternoon. When Georgy arrived, Anna was already sitting at a table outside, studying the menu. "Hey." He said as he slid onto the chair opposite her. "Hey yourself." She responded, waggling her eyebrows over her sunglasses. The place was packed with students and passers-by alike and it took a while for the waitress to get to their table.

The lady who ended up taking their order looked nothing like the strange man Georgy had seen at school in January. She was short, rotund with bleach-blond hair – and a woman. "Can I get ya' anything?" She asked, tapping her scratchpad for emphasis. "Two cups of coffee and two sandwiches, please. Egg salad. George?" "Uh, sure." Georgy gave an awkward cough. He was pretty sure that the waitress rolled her eyes when she turned her back on them. "You, uh, you like coffee?" He asked. Anna who had just put the menu neatly back into its place gave him a thumbs up. Georgy looked at his hands. They lay in his lap folded and sweaty. He didn't like coffee

191

and he hadn't imagined himself drinking it, at least not for the next five years or so. He glanced at Anna, completely at ease where she sat. She was watching a well-dressed man and woman one table over.

Georgy couldn't help but wonder: How long would she stick with him? He pushed his feet under his chair to hide his worn-out sneakers. "You think it's the waitress." She whispered in his direction with her best faux-scandalized face. Georgy rolled his eyes. "Don't think she would have fit through the bathroom window." He looked the waitress up and down when she rounded the corner laden with trays. "Seriously though." He said. "Hair is all wrong. Shoes, too." "What about the hair? It's been a while since you saw the guy, right? Could have gotten a haircut." She leaned in a little closer. "I mean, she's obviously a woman and all, but just in theory." Georgy avoided Anna's eyes. Instead of looking at her, he busied himself scratching some dirt off the table. "She doesn't have a lot of money." He said. It was meant to sound like a statement but somehow came out like a question. "My mom dyes her hair – and after a few weeks it looks like that. With the grey peeking out and the color fading. And her shoes..." He self-consciously pushed his own even further under his seat. "Well, they look like she's been wearing them for a while." "Regular Sherlock Holmes, aren't you?" She said, grinning at him over her sunglasses. Georgy forced a smile. He had experience with those sorts of things, was all. There was nothing

192

special about it. His jaw set. "Considering all the business he gets from our school alone, our friend probably doesn't have money troubles. True." Anna said, looking back over at the pretty couple next to them.

"Amy! Don't tell me you forgot about table four!" It was a man's voice, coming from somewhere behind the bar. Georgy couldn't see the speaker from where he was sitting. "S'cuse me." Anna had already gotten up, readjusting the sunglasses on her face. "I'll be back in a moment. If I'm not back in a few minutes..." "I'll come get you."

Georgy watched her move across the room. Her clothes were definitely not second-hand, that was obvious. He shrugged. He wasn't about to be able to afford anything better than he was already wearing – and even if he had more money, he certainly wouldn't spend it on clothes. Anna doesn't mind, he told himself. So why should he?

Anna returned shortly after looking excited. "Ponytail and brown hair." She said. "What do you think? Do you want to look at him for yourself?" Georgy shrugged. He knew he wouldn't be able to recognize the Frenchman's face, even if he saw it. "Was he wearing a suit?" He asked doubtfully. Anna chuckled. "Yes." She said. "But there weren't any tears in it, as far as I could tell." "Oh." Well, now what? Georgy found it was hard to meet her eyes again. He was supposed to be the idea guy. Anna probably expected him to know what to do and here he was drawing a complete- "Don't worry. I've got a plan." His eyes shot up to look at her. "It's not really subtle – I'm still finding my style." "Go ahead." Georgy said. "Ferdinand Bleriot, the principal's brother." Anna hummed, twirling a strand of hair around her finger.

"Lovely name, innit?"
"Yeah. So?"
"Good name. French name."
"*Yeah. So?*"
"Gotta love the French. Good food. The wine-"
"Anna."
"Hey, don't rush me. You do this every time you have a plan." Georgy felt himself blushing. "No, I don't!" He stuttered but Anna just waved dismissively. "No, no, I get it." She said. "It's hilarious." Georgy scowled. Anna giggled.
"So I was thinking: If we tell Kevin we know who he gets his stuff from – picture a nice day in the classroom: Sun's out, not a cloud in the sky-"
"*Anna.*"
"All right, all right. Basically, if we are correct, Kevin will probably lose it when we say the guy's name."

The waitress brought their food. Georgy wolfed down his sandwich, listening to Anna going on about this and that and even tried a bit of coffee. It was about as gross as he had expected but luckily Anna limited herself to one joke at his expense, before she ordered him some hot cocoa. They sat there a while longer, talking and just when they had found out that they both didn't like the Roadrunner cartoons, the waitress came back.

"You guys need anything else?" "Nope, we're all set for now." Georgy grinned. "Check please." Said Anna. Turning to George, she went on: "So the objective..." He rolled his eyes. "Is to catch Kevin off guard, right? Can you handle that?" Georgy snorted. There was no way he was that obnoxious. "Hold your horses greenhorn. This isn't my first rodeo." "Hey now!" She said warmly and leaned over to kiss the tip of his nose. "Your girlfriend is having a good time. Don't be such a killjoy." Georgy blushed again, though for different reasons. Defeated but smiling he heaved a sigh. "Beg your pardon m'am. What's the plan again?"

On Monday morning Georgy had just finished telling the others of their plan when Kevin arrived, looking shifty as ever. He shuffled over to his seat without giving them so much as a second look – which was all the cue they needed. With a curt nod in his direction, Georgy and Raff got up from where they sat and marched over to Kevin like nobody's business. "What do you want?" Kevin hissed once they were within whispering-distance. "So. You get your deliveries from Ferdinand, huh? Does the principal know about this?" Georgy asked nonchalantly as if they were talking about the weather. "Is he in on it?" Raff added. Georgy knew that they had hit the jackpot before Kevin got out so much as a peep by the way his eyes widened. "Who told you that?" He rasped. "You did. Just now." Kevin swallowed audibly. "How about..." Georgy went on, still doing his best to sound friendly. "We tell him that you're a rat." "That you're telling everyone where you get your stuff all willy-nilly. Just for fun?" Kevin's face had turned the color of freshly pressed chalk and they turned to leave. "Remember." Georgy said in passing. "Be good now."

"Well, I'd call that a success." Georgy announced during recess. "We finally know who the Frenchman is." "Yeah, yeah time to celebrate and all that." Wally said, rolling his eyes. "But that guy is gonna get himself a new dealer if Kevin ducks out. Sure as anything." "Don't care as long as he doesn't try to recruit me." Raff shrugged. "Good for you." Anna grumbled, glaring at Raff. "It's not like that guy is a violent psycho who makes kids harass each other for money and one less beating." "Okay, easy there. I didn't mean it like that." "So someone else we have to make go away." Georgy said pensively. Wally rolled his eyes. "It's an adult though. Telling his parents would be a weak threat." "Most adults aren't smarter than we are, I think." Lisa said soothingly. "Yeah, who in their right mind would hire Philip and Kevin to do their dirty work?" Georgy added, grinning. All eyes were suddenly on George. "So ..."Wally said dryly. "Any bright ideas?" Georgy felt a hot rush of anger.

196

"We'd have to lure him into a trap." He snapped. "Then the police show up and catch him." "I get the feeling I heard that somewhere before." Georgy glared at Wally. "So? You got a better plan?" Wally shrugged. "And how are we going to do that?" Asked Urs, dangling from Raff's arm. "You don't have anything on him, like you did on Philip; like the painting." "Or a brain." Anna commented off-handedly but the next moment her face fell and she clapped her hands. "You're smart." She cooed. "Uh, thanks?" It wasn't that Georgy didn't appreciate the comment – it was more so that not knowing what she was getting at didn't make him feel smart at all. "No, listen..." Anna leaned in conspiratorially. "Bleriot hired Philip and Kevin even though they are..." "As bright as a wet match in a dark basement?" Raff supplied helpfully. "So you're saying I should get that guy to hire me? Huh."

Georgy thought about that for a moment. "I could write him a letter, I guess. That I got Phil and Kev out of the way so I could sell the stuff myself." Raff whistled. "If there ever was any doubt that you were crazy..." "Don't worry, it's all a ruse." Said Lisa. "I know that!" Raff's neck was turning a splotchy shade of red. "That's not the point!" "What Raff's trying to say..." Wally clasped a hand over Raff's shoulder. "Is: What if you just end up making the guy mad and getting yourself killed in the process?" "That won't happen." Georgy said defiantly. "I'll be careful." For the fraction of a second, something like actual anger flashed across Wally's face, then he looked away. "I'll write that I'd like to meet on the old playground by the forest. If he shows, we know that we have him hooked. Then the negotiations can begin. Anna, I'll need you there to take pictures from cover." Anna nodded. "I'll also ask him to bring some stuff that I can try and sell. Now, ideally you'll take a picture when he hands it over and... Maybe try and get and angle where you can crop out my face?"

"Once that's done with, I guess we'll talk about when we'll meet again. And then I'll send the stuff to the police, picture and everything, like a present from Ferdinand." Georgy finished with a flourish of his hand, unable to strike the self-satisfaction from his voice entirely. "Then they'll just have to bust him the next time we made an exchange." "You should go to the police now." Wally deadpanned. "Not put Anna in danger for chance to play hero." That threw Georgy for a loop. For a full ten seconds, he didn't have the foggiest idea how to respond to that – other than the sudden and almost overwhelming urge to break Wally's nose again. "You said it yourself." He finally bit out. "Those people will believe everything they see. Chances are that they just aren't going to believe unless we take them by the neck and force them to look. I'm not gonna risk that asshole getting away because some officer doesn't take us seriously, takes forever to get a search warrant and ends up tipping him off. No. We go to the police when we have all the proof we need and then some." They glared at each other for a moment but instead of subsiding, the tension only seemed to escalate. "Hey, hey, you guys..." Raff shrugged off Urs' arm and went to stand between the two of them, uncomfortably shifting from one foot to the other. "This is isn't about my ego." Georgy hissed. Wally glared him down. "This is because I don't see another way."

Everyone fell quiet after that, distracted by their own thoughts. Georgy slipped into a downward spiral of envisioning terrible scenarios in which one thing after the other went wrong. He looked at Anna who was biting the inside of her cheek and it felt like his stomach was turning into lead.

"So..." After school, he was sitting on a bench next to Anna. "Any plans for the summer?" She asked. "Anywhere in particular your family wants to go?" Georgy, who was still caught up in thoughts of what could go wrong with his plan (there were just so many things), took a while to process what had just been said. "Uh, vacation, summer, right..." Then he made a decision – why lie? Anna was cool, she didn't care about money and they were friends. He took a deep breath and plucked up his courage. "Uhm, you know... My family doesn't do trips. Other than the odd weekend camping trip to some, like cheap..." He stopped himself, blushed abruptly and gave her a shaky smile. "Frame of reference: Other than moving, I've never left the state." Anna said nothing, just listened. She probably sensed that he wasn't finished. "I asked my dad – Stepdad." He corrected himself. "If maybe I could work at his workshop during summer break. I could make up to... over 1500 bucks working there for two months." Anna nodded slowly. Maybe he was imagining it, but she looked a little sad. "Hey, cheer up." He said, doing his best to reinforce the smile that was starting to slip. "I mean, I need to be able to afford that ice cream I owe you somehow. I guess maybe I could steal it but you know how-" She silenced him with a kiss. "I'll be spending that time in Venice. We have a house there." "How many weeks will you be gone?" "All of them. Just me and Arty." "Oh." Georgy mumbled. "So we won't see each other for a while." Anna nodded. "Seems that way." They sat there for a few moments. Anna's fingers grazed his and he carefully took her hand. "You know I don't care about that stuff." She whispered. "The money and all that. I'd move into that nook behind the curtain in your room right now, if I could." For the second time that day, Georgy was completely taken aback. He didn't rightly know what to say to that; nothing he could come up with seemed appropriate. He settled on. "I'll write you every day, if you want." They looked into each other's eyes. "But only if you write back." He added meaningfully, hoping that Anna would be able to feel his sincerity. "You're sweet." She muttered. He kissed her.

"Okay, change of subject." He announced as he pulled back. Anna rolled her eyes. "That writing thing. Could you get on that, like, sooner rather than later?" "Don't tell me you are going to prison." "No." Now it was Georgy's turn to roll his eyes. "Just - could you use your mom's typewriter to type a letter for me?" He couldn't help but cross his fingers behind his back. "Sure. Just tell me what to write." Anna gave him a smile, mischievous and bashful at once. "Um, okay." He muttered. Well, that had been easy. Briefly, he wondered what had changed but when Anna pulled some paper and a pen from her pocket and looked at him expectantly, he pushed the thought to the back of his mind and began to dictate.

,Weird.' He thought on his way home. His mind kept coming back to the plan. He'd pretended to be confident with Wally, sure. Because Wally had chosen the most ridiculously bad moment to turn into gigantic- Georgy shook his head. But still. Was this worth putting Anna at risk? This was for her, he thought. It was what she wanted, what she said she wanted. She loved this kind of stuff! Images of Wally's bruised face, covered in bandages, his crooked nose made an unbidden entrance in Georgy's mind. He imagined Anna looking that way, remembered her face after her brother had beaten her up. Wally had been there when he'd first seen her. He brought his bike to a sudden stop. What if Anna would be the same as Wally? What if she'd suddenly start avoiding him, if every word out of his mouth would end up making her mad. That moment, Georgy wished that she were on the plane to Miami already.

201

I have to do this, he thought. I have to do this so I'll be able to think clearly again.

The next day he slipped the letter into the Bistro's mailbox. Two days later, he'd meet the guy on the playground.

Raff and Urs had gotten in to position. Anna was hiding behind a bush, ready to snap some pictures if needed. Her dad owned a rather impressive collection of photography equipment she could 'borrow' from whenever she wanted, especially since the guy only seemed to be home once in a blue moon. The other two were pretending to have a romantic evening some distance away. At least Georgy hoped that they were pretending. He needed Raff and Urs alert in case something happened, not tongue-deep in each other's throats. Gross. George was waiting on a swing, quietly hoping that no more people would show up. One woman had left mere minutes ago, two wailing children in tow. He had picked the time in hopes that most kids would be home for dinner when Ferdinand arrived. His mother would probably be expecting him too, had he not told her that he was going to have dinner at Raff's.

A green car pulled onto the nearby parking lot. Georgy glanced into the direction of the dying engine and immediately recognized Ferdinand. He was alone. Georgy heaved a relieved sigh. Had the Frenchman brought back up, Georgy would have given the order to evacuate immediately. Hand gesture. Not order.

His heart was beating frantically against his ribs, like a bird trying to escape a cage. Apparently, it didn't really want to be there either. That thought almost made him laugh. Instead, he slowly rose from his seat and gave Ferdinand a slight nod. The Frenchman sauntered toward him, slowly. Deliberately. And entirely at easy. He came to a stop directly in front of George, gave him a lazy once-over and lit a cigarette.

"Fancy yourself a businessman, do ya boy?" He said quietly without giving George a second glance. Georgy felt a growing lump in his throat. He could not help but lean in a little more to make out what the man was saying. He noticed that his knees were shaking. The Frenchman turned his head ever so slightly, his eyes meeting Georgy's and he quirked a questioning brow. "Y-yes. Yes, I do." The Frenchman sniffed and Georgy couldn't help but marvel at how collected he seemed. Was this really the same man he'd seen attacking Philip not that long ago? "So you want to sell for me, pipsqueak?" Georgy just so managed to get a grasp before the silence dragged on too long. "The 'Pipsqueak'." He sneered. "Did away with your other guys, in case you hadn't noticed. If you don't believe me, I'll gladly tell you exactly how I did it. How I tricked Philip with the drugs and the painting and how I blew up Kevin's flowers."

The Frenchman smiled mirthlessly. "That was you, was it? Word of advice, boy: Don't go around telling

203

random strangers about your criminal history." Georgy could feel the blood shooting up through his neck and into his face. "You lost me good money there." The Frenchman went on like he hadn't noticed. "It's been weeks since any significant quantities have been moved at that school of yours." Georgy realized how angry the man was. "And that's exactly why I'm gonna do it in their stead. Naturally, I had to get rid of them first, though. Otherwise you wouldn't have had a reason to take me on." The Frenchman scoffed. "And why would I take you on now? You screwed me." "Yeah, I screwed you but I'm smart. Smarter than those two morons at any rate." "Why? You a pothead?" "Money." Georgy said in a clipped voice and gestured at his worn sneakers. "I just want the money." The Frenchman gave a slow nod. "Ah, very well. Then..." He pulled something from his pocket. "This is for you." He dropped the bundle in Georgy's hand. It was wrapped in brown paper. "Consider it a gift of opportunity. What you do with this is entirely your decision. In two weeks, we will meet again and then maybe..." The Frenchman made a vague gesture. "You will have a gift for me." "A gift of opportunity?" Georgy drawled laconically. "150 dollars in cash. If you happen to have something more, well, that is good for you, no?" 150 dollars. That was a lot. Georgy suddenly realized that he had never sold anything in his life, let alone anything drugs. He hadn't even had a lemonade stand before. "Keep it for now." He said. "I have people waiting for me at home and explaining your gift to them may prove difficult.

Monday evening, same place, same time." For a brief moment, Ferdinand gaped at him, then his mouth curled into a thin-lipped smile. "You're not a pothead but you're still a junkie, eh? What's your game?" Ferdinand's eyes narrowed like he was scanning him. "If you don't want to do this, that works for me too." Georgy said with a shrug. His heart was hammering away frantically. When Ferdinand didn't respond, didn't even move, Georgy turned around and walked toward his bike. Just as he had expected, Ferdinand called out to him. "You just tell complete stranger you cause property damage for fun and then you walk away?" Georgy prayed that the playground really was as deserted as he thought it was. "Bad habit." He muttered and looked at Ferdinand over his shoulder. Ferdinand chuckled again. "You're different." He said. "I like the, as you say, cut of your jib." Ferdinand pulled something out of his pocket that looked like a small notebook or a pocket calendar. He flipped it open. "Monday evening." He said, wrote it down and looked at Georgy. "You better show up. You set the time, so you wouldn't want to – inconvenience – me." "I'll be there, you can rely on that." And so would be some nice gentlemen in uniforms. "See you then." Georgy said as he got onto his bike. "Dinner is waiting."

Once he had rounded the corner, he got off his bike and took a few deep breaths. He sat on the curb and stared at his hands. They were shaking. This had already been bad enough, how would things go when the police were arrived?

Georgy had no idea how long he just sat there, waiting for nothing in particular, when Anna came hurtling toward him. "Awesome! She exclaimed. "Awesome terrifying awesomeness!" Raff and Urs appeared behind her. "We had to wait until the French guy was gone." Raff said by way of explanation. "Once you had left he just stood there smoking his cigarette." Raff shook his head. "I thought he had caught on to why we were there or something." "I've taken so many pictures!" Anna said excitedly. "That's great." Georgy mumbled. "Considering how convinced I was that this whole thing was going to blow up in my face." He gave her a shaky smile. "Good to know it wasn't for nothing." Once Georgy had brought the others up to speed, they discussed how things were supposed to go on Monday. "I'll have the pictures developed by Saturday. I'll have the letter typed out by then, too." "Sounds great. We'll be able to drop everything off at the precinct at once." "What will we do if they're a no-show?" Raff asked doubtfully. "Then we walk right in there and confront them with the evidence."

On his way to Anna's house, Georgy had picked some flowers off the side of the road. After he had had the customary awkward exchange with Arty at the doorstep, Anna was already waiting for him. She was wearing a pretty dress and her hair in a ponytail.

He felt a little silly when he handed her the flowers, but she regaled him with the most charming of smiles and the feeling quickly faded.

"Thank you." She whispered. "There's somebody I want you to meet." Georgy followed her into the entrance hall. There were a man and a woman waiting there for them. Georgy immediately felt like his stomach had turned into lead. "My parents." Anna said by way of explanation. Her smile seemed a little strained. The woman approached him without moment's hesitation and extended a hand. She gave him a once-over and smiled. "So you're that good-for-nothing little rascal Anna has told us so much about." Georgy willed himself to say something, anything, but his tongue seemed to have quit the field. It was dangling uselessly somewhere between the back of his throat and his stomach. Misses Dasher didn't seem to care though. She leaned in and pulled him into a very tight – and very unexpected – hug. "My, but you are cute." She smelled like what Georgy guessed was incredibly expensive perfume. "Now, now, honey." Mister Dasher said good-naturedly. "The poor boy may never sleep again." Georgy threw Anna a panicked glance. She shrugged, pretended to gag and gave him a thumbs up in quick succession. He had no idea what it all meant but it calmed him all the same. "Nice to meet you, Mister and Miss's Dasher. I'm George." Mister Dasher clasped a hand over his shoulder. "You're the man of the hour, George. We have you to thank for taking care of our little dumpling-pie, don't we." Georgy gaped at the man like he had never seen another person before. Dumpling-what now?

Anna noisily cleared her throat and the hint of color on her cheeks suggested that she didn't appreciate her dad's choice of words. "They, uh, they just wanted to meet you for themselves." She said and gave her dad a venomous glare. Mister Dasher chuckled softly and raised his hands in mock-defense. "We need to thank you appropriately." Said Misses Dasher and squeezed his hand. She was an exceptionally beautiful woman with vibrant blue eyes and long black hair just like Anna's. Only at her temples, there was a thin line of grey and the creases around her eyes didn't vanish when she relaxed her face. "Is there something we can do for you?" She asked and he felt a little like he was meeting the wizard of OZ. "Uh, no, not really." He stammered. Mister Dasher finally took his hand of Georgy's shoulder. "How about dinner then?"

Chapter 10 Going out with a bang

Fifteen minutes. Georgy was sitting on the swing again, just like last time. He looked around and couldn't help but wonder why the place was absolutely deserted. Had the police already cleared everybody out? His friends were nowhere to be seen. Georgy was pulling on his fingers. What if the police wouldn't be there at all? Kind of a gross oversight that that was even a possibility. On the other hand, if things went south he could always just take the stuff like a good little dealer and go to the police again afterwards. They'd have to believe him eventually – even if it was at the stage where he was in a hospital bed somewhere, because Ferdinand suddenly no longer liked t*he cut of his jib.* It was a different car that pulled up next to the playground this time. The doors opened and Ferdinand stepped outside, followed by another man. *Oh, no.* Georgy thought, and a feeling of ice-cold dread settled in his stomach – but it was already too late.

It wasn't even six yet. He managed a short glance at the other man from the corner of his eye and noticed some movement behind the car. Probably one of his friends, trying to get a closer look. God damn risky and stupid. He clenched his fists by his sides. Georgy looked over again, trying to look as inconspicuous as possible so the men approaching him wouldn't notice. It was Anna. What did she think she was doing?! And where was the police?

209

"You're here on time. I like that." The Frenchman drawled. "This is August, a very well-connected friend of mine. Play your cards right and he may become one of yours, too." "Don't count on it." August grumbled. In a louder voice, he went on: "Any idea where you'll be hidin' the stuff, boy? Fred tells me yer bright." "In an old barn behind our house. In the hayloft. Nobody uses it so nobody will find it." It was a complete lie and Georgy was a little surprised how easily it rolled off his tongue. He peaked at his watch. "Got somewhere too be again, eh? Busy, busy man?" "No, why?" "Your watch. Or are you making sure it's still there." Georgy shook his head, just as if he were surprised himself. Where in the blazes was the police? "How will you be transporting the stuff?" "Backpack." He muttered, dejectedly throwing a hand over his shoulder. Ferdinand scoffed, apparently marginally less impressed with that than the barn thing. Still, he indicated for his friend to go over to their car. *Damn it, Anna, get out of there.* When August returned to them, digging around in a bag he was now carrying, a patrol car rounded the corner and rolled onto the parking lot.

"Shit!" The Frenchman screamed. "You screwed us, you little bastard." Gone was any trace of refinement, as he lunged toward George. "Police! En avant!" He yelled at August. The other man spun around on his heel and drew his pistol from the holster. "Merde alors. Emporte lui!" Georgy heard a click and his insides turned into a knot when he realized that it had been the gun's safety coming off. "No!" He screamed, when August threw up his arms, swayed on the spot for a moment, then steadied himself, aimed at the police car and opened fire. With a jolt, Georgy felt himself being dragged forward and almost fell over his own legs. The Frenchman's vice grip around his waist only tightened as he forced him forward, toward the car. Georgy stared at the gun, a thin line of smoke rising from the barrel. For a brief moment, he almost forgot that he was supposed to be fighting but it was pointless. The Frenchman was far stronger than him. August had hit the right front wheel. "Merde, il y a deux enfants!". He had discovered Anna, cowering behind the Frenchman's car like she had been paralyzed. Without wasting a second, he had her by the collar and carelessly tossed her into the car like a ragdoll. The policemen had taken cover behind their own vehicle. "No. No!" Georgy croaked, trying desperately to twist his way out of the Frenchman's arms. With a cry of outrage, the Frenchman tripped him, a hand between his shoulder blades and drove him into the car's sidewall headfirst. A sharp pain shot all the way down to his neck and the world began to spin. He vaguely registered that his face was cushioned by something soft, that the engine roared to life like an abused animal – then everything turned black.

When he opened his eyes, a bright, clinical light was shining directly in his face and he immediately screwed them shut. His head hurt and he was confused. It took a moment before he remembered what had happened. He snapped into an upright position and regretted it almost immediately. There was a pounding sensation like something was trying to force its way out of the back of his skull. He carefully ran a hand across his temples and looked around. "Don't worry. You're not bleeding." Anna. For the second time in a row, he looked around to quickly and was almost overwhelmed by nausea. "A-Are you okay?" He managed and quickly pressed a sleeve onto his mouth. She nodded. Her face was uncharacteristically pale and her eyes were puffy. "But you're not. I tried to tell them that you needed a doctor." Her voice grew faint as she spoke. "I'm fine." He said, trying to make it sound convincing, while slowly leaning back against a shelf. He had barely moved and still he was feeling motion sickness like he had just gotten off a roller coaster. "We didn't drive that far." She told him. "Maybe ten minutes. Four miles, at most." Georgy relaxed a little. That meant that they couldn't be further away than one of the neighboring villages.

The relief appeared to have been visible on his face, because Anna dejectedly shook her head. "Door's locked and I doubt that we'll be able to beat it down." Georgy looked around, moving his head at a deliberately slow pace. The last thing he needed was to throw up all over himself. The floor seemed to consist of compressed soil. The ceiling was made up of a few earthy alcoves, the walls were lined with twee-sacks, and preserve jars. "What is this place?" He asked. "A barn, I think." Georgy made to get to his feet but Anna already had a hand on his shoulder. "Don't." She breathed. "You're in no shape to be walking around." Georgy looked into her eyes, ready to disagree, to argue. But she was right. He could barely sit, how was he supposed to get them out of there? He felt something wet on his face and started at the realization that it was a tear. "I'm sorry." He whispered and lowered his head onto his hands. "This- this..." He pressed his lips into a tight line. He didn't see a way out. Nobody knew where they were. If the police searched for them, would they find them?

And would they still be alive if they were found? The weight of Anna's hand hadn't left his shoulder. "At least we won't starve." She said weakly. "How do you feel about pickles for dinner." Georgy half-laughed, half-sobbed in response. "Of course there will also be pickles for breakfast tomorrow, so we have that to look forward to." She went on and then added, in a steadier voice: "I'll get us out of here."

She got to her feet, walked over to the big door at the far side of the room and peered through the keyhole. "No key. They probably took it with them. There's a staircase leading up, the lights are on so they are either still here or just really wasteful." She chuckled mirthlessly at her own joke, just when there was a sound like a door slamming shut upstairs. "You think they're gone?" She whispered. "Maybe." Georgy mumbled. He had read somewhere that you weren't supposed to sleep after getting a concussion but he was just so tired.

Anna was looking through the shelves. Georgy lowered his head onto his knees and closed his eyes. "I'm sorry, Anna." He muttered. Anna ignored him, opting instead to list whatever she saw on the shelves. "Sugar, salt, potatoes. More potatoes. Oh, look. Seems like they're already hording firework supplies for the fourth of July." "I shouldn't have gotten you involved in this. We should have just gone straight to the police." "Toolkit, charcoal, an old lawn-mower." "Wally was right, if I hadn't-" "Now listen here, bucko. First of all, you didn't *get me involved in this,* I decided to be here. Second, I'm getting real tired of your pessimism, so you can be helpful or you can be quiet."

Georgy slowly opened his eyes. He was sitting on a bag of Weedex. Main ingredient: Potassium chlorate. "Wait." He said. "Firework supplies?" "Yes." Anna grumbled. "How about firecrackers?" "Yes." She sounded far less aggravated now, almost excited. He heard her tear open the plastic packaging. She went over to the door again and crouched down in front of it. "It fits." She exclaimed. "The firecracker fits into the keyhole. "That won't be enough." Georgy groaned, starting another ill-fated attempt to get to his feet. He

214

stumbled and fell forward. "Shit." He hissed. "Damn it." Again, there was a pressure on his shoulder as Anna heaved him into a sitting position. "I fit right in with all the other potato sacks." He joked. "The resemblance is astonishing." She beamed. "Now tell me   what   to   do."

He instructed Anna to find some powdered sugar, which she poured into a bowl previously filled by a bunch of bent nails. Then he watched her tear open the Weedex and add it to the sugar. Lastly, she pulled him top of one of the firecrackers and combined everything with the black powder. "Now put as much of that as you can fit on a tissue, roll it up and stick it into the keyhole. Then take another firecracker and stick it in after. Once you've lit it, you better get back here   as   fast   as   possible   and   cover   your ears." Seconds later, there was a hissing noise, Anna barreled toward him, her eyes already closed in anticipation, her hands covering her ears. There was a loud bang that resonated throughout the entire room and the two of them were showered by a rain of woodchips. Georgy cracked open an eye that he hadn't realized he had closed. Half the room was obscured by thick black smoke. If the door didn't open now, there was a good chance they would suffocate. A cough wrecked his body with enough force to make his head hurt again. "Here we go." Anna wheezed somewhere next to him and hauled him to his feet. Georgy cursed, as she dragged him more than carried him toward the door. The heavy scent of

215

black powder and burnt wood was biting his nose.

Looking back, Georgy couldn't remember how exactly Anna had managed to get him up the stairs or into the yard. The Frenchman and his friend were nowhere to be seen as they wobbled over to the street. He knew where they were now. Ferdinand had just taken them to the village he went to school in. "So what now?" He croaked.   "It would probably be best if you just left me here for a moment and-" "No chance." Anna ground out, dragging him along. "You wouldn't leave me here either." "Anna, you should just ring someone's doorbell and-" "Bossy. Can you reach into my back pocket." Georgy did as she told him, if only because he was so taken aback by how resolutely she was disagreeing with him. He found a small key. "No way." He breathed. "Yep." She let go of him and he steadied himself against Ferdinand's car. "Get in, my lady." She said as she unlocked it. "We have places to be." "You stole his car keys?!" "Hey, I told you I was finding my style."

Anna dropped him off at the hospital even though he protested as good as he got, then she left for the police station, promising that he'd get some news soon. Apparently, the policemen had already gotten most they had needed to know from Raff, Urs and Olly and only grumbled something about more paperwork because Anna had technically stolen a car. They were, however, quite impressed to because apparently people who got kidnapped usually didn't drive themselves home.

The next day, Georgy was sitting in his hospital bed, surrounded by friends and family, his own and everyone else's, while Urs was reading the newspaper to them. *"Young detectives make short work of seasoned criminals."*

"Yesterday evening a group of local teenagers, in co-operation with the police, managed to put a stop to the illegal dealings of a drug cartel that had a hand in supplying most of the state with marijuana. A police representative informed reporters that the main suspect, Ferdinand B., had been under surveillance for the better part of the last year, only to culminate in a dramatic showdown yesterday evening. He and his associate will be tried within the coming days.
The teenagers who contributed to detaining the criminals will likely receive commendations within the coming weeks."

Georgy's mother incredulously stared at him. "You did that?" Georgy avoided her eyes and rubbed his head. "Well, not by myself." Anna had brought him a bunch of flowers and was now holding his hand, quietly smiling to herself. "Thank god nothing happened to you." His mother muttered and for a moment, he was sure that their eyes were unusually light. She sniveled into a handkerchief and his dad put his arm around her. "I'm proud of you." He said. "Of all of you." He nodded at Raff and Urs, Anna and Olly. "Where's Walter?" He asked. "Sends his best." Raff shrugged. There was a knock on the door and Georgy's little brother darted over to open it. "May we come in?" It was Mister and Misses Dasher. "Uh, sure. They are Anna's parents." He told his mother. It took quite a bit of tuning, and even more quiet grumbling from Georgy's roommate, until everybody had managed to fit into the room semi-comfortably. "Well, son, I'm sure you're wondering why we're here." Georgy saw his father roll his eyes and had to fight a smile. "Yes, Sir." He said. "You're all little heroes." Misses Dasher exclaimed and threw her hands around the neck of the person closest to her, which just so happened to be Olly who bushed furiously. "And we wanted to thank you for all you have done for our daughter." Georgy shrugged. "I don't know." He mumbled sheepishly. "I think we're pretty   even."

"Yes? Well, we'd still like to extend an invitation for you to come join us on our summer vacation to Italy." Mister Dasher quickly turned to Georgy's parents. "Only if you would allow it, of course." "Your vacation to where?" Georgy's mom said haltingly. "We have a summer residence in Venice." Misses Dasher said by way of explanation. "Anna will be spending the summer there and learning a little Italian along the way." "Fingers crossed." Mister Dasher grinned. "George would be welcome to accompany her

218

and brush up on European culture as well." Georgy glanced at his hands folded in his lap. "May I?" He asked carefully. "Well..." Georgy's mom looked at his dad. "I-I don't see a reason why not, so..." "It's settled then!" Mister Dasher produced a bottle of champagne, seemingly out of nowhere. "A toast to our little heroes!" Anna threw George a kiss.

END